D1518268

FAITHFUL TO A DREAM

Beth was fiercely loyal to Charles Stuart as he fought to regain his dead father's throne, even though it brought her into conflict with Tom Everard, the man she was growing to love. Her desire to help the would-be king brought her danger and disillusionment. Reality did not match her dreams, but Tom was there to help her and to teach her how to find happiness in a country divided by civil war.

SHEILA HOLROYD

FAITHFUL TO A DREAM

Complete and Unabridged

LINFORD
Leicester

First published in Great Britain in 1997

First Linford Edition
published 2006

British Library CIP Data

Holroyd, Sheila
    Faithful to a dream.—Large print ed.—
Linford romance library
    1. Great Britain—History—Civil War,
1642 – 1649 —Fiction
    2. Love stories 3. Large type books
    I. Title
    823.9′14 [F]

ISBN 1–84617–377–9

Published by
F. A. Thorpe (Publishing)
Anstey, Leicestershire

Set by Words & Graphics Ltd.
Anstey, Leicestershire
Printed and bound in Great Britain by
T. J. International Ltd., Padstow, Cornwall

This book is printed on acid-free paper

1

Beth's eyes blazed with fury as she stood on the dusty field path and her words gave vent to her anger.

'How dare you tell me what I can say and do!'

The young man looked at her grimly.

'Someone has to tell you to guard your tongue.'

'You used to be my friend, Tom Everard! Now all you do is find fault with me.'

She clenched her fists as if almost ready to attack him.

He sighed with exasperation. How could he make her see that she must watch what she said?

'Do you want the old woman to be hanged as a witch?' he said brutally.

Beth's eyes widened with shock as she stared up at his stern face, and her voice faltered. She tucked a lock of ebony-dark hair back under her cap.

'But I only said that Granny Walsh was telling me stories about fairies and elves. Why should she be thought a witch?'

'Because England, in the Year of Our Lord 1651, is now a godly common-wealth, and people who talk about such heathen rubbish cannot be good Christians.'

'Granny Walsh says it isn't rubbish,' Beth returned defiantly. 'She said she knows there are still fairies because they sometimes leave a rabbit on her doorstep at night as a present to a believer.'

'Beth, don't tell anyone else what she said.' Tom gave a startled frown. 'Do you realise that if people heard nonsense like that they would be sure to seize her as a witch, and you'd be responsible for her death!'

'Do you really think it could happen?'

He nodded firmly as she looked up at him pleadingly.

'Even now, there are fools who will kill people they fear because they do not understand them.'

Beth placed a confiding hand on the sleeve of his jacket.

'But I can say what I like to you, can't I, Tom? You won't repeat what I say?'

'Beth Henchley, you know you can say anything and I'll keep it secret. What matters is not what I think but what Parliament and its army think.'

'Of course. I know what you mean. There's always somebody anxious to show how godly they are by reporting their neighbour's mistakes, though I didn't think an old woman's stories would cause trouble. But sometimes it's very difficult to watch every word I say and try not even to think about how different life could be.'

They resumed their walk, temporarily depressed at the complexities of life. Beth looked sideways at Tom under her long, curling lashes.

'Granny Walsh also said . . . '

He gave her a warning glare.

'But I'm only telling you what she remembered! She said that at Christmas there used to be feasting and singing, and people dancing throughout the kingdom! Why can't we have such revelries?'

Her amazement at the thought of such excitement animated her young face and brought colour to her clear skin.

'I don't believe a little enjoyment will send us all to Hell, and I don't believe you do either! Tom, wouldn't you like to wear velvet and satins in bright colours, and wear a sword and challenge people to duels?'

'I certainly don't want to fight anyone, and I don't think velvet and satin would be hardwearing enough when I'm helping to get the harvest in,' he replied repressively.

Then he looked at her thoughtfully. Her unadorned grey dress might have made most girls look drab, but its very lack of colour emphasised the dark lustre of her hair and outlined her slender figure.

'They might suit you better than me,' he commented.

Imperiously she waved him to a halt, and then walked round him slowly with studied deliberation, as she inspected him from head to toe.

For eight years Beth had been used to the company of his tall, gangling figure, but now, as she looked him over carefully, she was aware that he was changing. The youth had become a man. Now six feet tall, he was reaching well-built maturity, although his sober brown suit and stout shoes gave him the look of a respectable farmer, and certainly did not show that he was the son of Sir Thomas Everard and heir to a comfortable estate. Nor did his face give much sign of gentle breeding.

His frank blue eyes gave attraction to a face marked by its good humour rather than any aristocratic distinction. Although a nobleman might have been careful to preserve the white complexion that marked his difference from the workers on the land, Tom was tanned by the summer sun.

No sign of her new awareness showed in the thoughtful frown with which she surveyed him as he stood waiting for her judgement. Finally she seemed to reach a decision. Shaking her head slowly, she gave an exaggerated sigh of regret.

'I think it's your nose,' she said pensively. 'It's too short. You need a more impressive nose for fine clothes.'

He shouted with indignant laughter, and she picked up her skirts and fled as he chased her to the next stile in mock anger. There she accepted his hand to help her over the stile.

The two of them walked on with the easy companionship born of long acquaintance until the path through the cornfields reached the gate of a small black and white house, scarcely more than a cottage, with a small patch of garden separating it from the road.

Here they paused, and Beth turned to Tom to take her farewell.

'Remember what I said,' he cautioned her. 'Keep a watch on your tongue, or you'll get yourself and others into trouble.'

'I am eighteen, Tom Everard, and not a complete fool. I'll remember what you said. I just think it is a pity that your brave, new Commonwealth is so virtuous that everything is dull, and there's no room for dreams.'

'There are worse things than dullness, Beth.'

He waved an arm at the fields they had just crossed.

'A few years ago this land was being devastated by civil war between King and Parliament. It cost your father his life. It had reduced you and your mother to poverty. Was that better than a peaceful country, with men free to tend the land and feed their families?'

Once again his commonsense made her dreams seem foolish. She could think of no reply, and stalked up the short path into the house, leaving Tom to go his thoughtful way through a nearby gate in a high wall which gave a view of a red-brick, Jacobean mansion.

Meanwhile Beth had gone to the cottage kitchen, where a plump woman was busy peeling vegetables. She gave Beth a reproving glance.

'Wandering through the fields again with Master Tom, young lady?'

'Don't tell me you are spying on me now as well as the minister, Mary!' Beth said irritably.

'Spying! All I had to do was look out of the window.'

'I regard Tom Everard as my brother,' she said primly, and then lost her dignity as she hugged the cook. 'Don't be silly, Mary! You know Tom thinks of me as a little sister who needs to be taken care of.'

'I know he does,' Mary said grimly, 'but you're eighteen now, Miss Beth, and you must behave like a lady at your age. Even Master Tom must realise that you are growing up, if he ever thinks of anything but crops and cattle. Now come and help me peel these carrots.'

'You won't tell Mother you saw me with Tom, will you? You know she thinks of the Everards almost as enemies because they are Puritans.'

Mary patted the girl's hand sympathetically.

'You know I won't say anything to upset your mother,' she said reassuringly. 'Heaven knows I've had enough practice in keeping things from her these past eight years since your father was killed.'

She was sorry for the problems the young girl faced, but knew there was little she could do to help. When Richard Henchley had been killed fighting for King Charles at Newbury in 1643, his wife's life had also ended in many ways. Richard Henchley's death had been followed by Parliament's confiscation of most of his estate and goods.

Destitution threatened until Sir Thomas Everard, a Puritan magistrate and a friend of her husband before religion and politics drove them apart, had taken Mistress Henchley and her ten-year-old daughter into his care. He had installed them in the small house near his own mansion, and let it be known that they had his protection.

Beth's nurse, Mary, had accompanied the two of them, and she remembered the desperate days after Richard Henchley's death. The other servants had deserted the penniless widow, and Mary had fought to keep the three of them warm and fed. Mistress Henchley had scarcely been aware of the daily problems.

She had been prostrate with grief, crying out to her dead husband until Mary had feared for her sanity. Mary remembered her joy when, on the eve of their eviction, Sir Thomas's carriage had rumbled to a halt outside the house and he had declared his intention of taking them home with him.

Mistress Henchley had been tenderly wrapped in furs for the journey and then carefully nursed back to physical health by Mary and Lady Everard. When she had recovered, she had at first tried to refuse favours from a Puritan, but then she had lapsed into an apathy from which she had rarely emerged during the succeeding years.

Now, eight years later, her husband had become idealised into a saintly figure for whose sake she spent hours in prayer each day. While Mary and Beth tried to cope with the problems of being impoverished Royalists in a stronghold of Puritanism, Mistress Henchley seemed to be gradually losing touch with day-to-day existence.

Sir Thomas Everard had taken charge of the widow's affairs, letting her think that there was enough money left to support them. Mary knew the truth, and she had told Beth when she thought the girl old enough.

'I sometimes wonder what Mother would do if she realised that we depend on the Everards for nearly everything,' Beth mused. 'It's just as well that all she thinks of is my father. I wish I could remember him more clearly. Was he really so perfect, Mary?'

Mary snorted, recalling some of Richard Henchley's less saintly activities.

'No more than any other man, my pet, but if it comforts her to turn him into a saint, then let her.'

Meanwhile, Tom had made his way to the stables of the large house, where he found his father inspecting a mare who had lost a shoe. Having discussed the necessary visit to the blacksmith, they made their way into the house. Sir Thomas could see something was troubling his son.

'I met Beth when I was coming back from Grigg's farm,' Tom said eventually. 'She'd been to see Granny Walsh, and the old woman has been filling her head with stories of the festivals there used to be in former times.'

'Not surprising,' his father commented. 'She's getting on for eighty, and at that age, memories of past times seem brighter than today.'

'That would be all very well, if Beth saw them as past times, but you know what she's like. She wants England ruled by a king, bishops running the church again, and she says so. That could be dangerous.'

'You're thinking of Minister Werham.' His father sighed and sat down.

Tom's silence was confirmation.

'I admit that the man is an unforgiving fanatic who hates all Royalists and their families, but he can do Beth no harm so long as she curbs her tongue in public. And she's a sensible girl, young as she is, and well-liked. A lot of people would be upset if Werham tried to harm her in any way.'

'She's a darling,' Tom said softly, 'when she's not being insufferable. Werham would have to face me if he tried any of his tricks. But did you have to give such an unpleasant man the living of Hatchford?'

'It would have been difficult for me

to reject him.' His father shrugged. 'He was recommended by some members of Parliament, and I'd already aroused enough suspicion by sheltering the family of a Royalist. With Worcester only thirty miles away, I sometimes feel I am being watched.'

The conversation was interrupted by the bustling entry of a middle-aged lady with blue eyes very like her son's.

'There you are at last, Tom. I've been busy with preserves all morning, and I'd be grateful if you'd take a few jars over to Mary this evening.'

'Gladly, Mother. Is there anything else?'

'They can't have much meat. Can we send them some mutton?' she enquired, looking at her husband.

'Send them anything that you think we can spare,' he returned.

'Sometimes it is the sending that is most difficult. Mistress Henchley would never knowingly accept charity from us. Tom and the girls have to take things across very discreetly.' She sighed.

'At times, Father, I'm not quite discreet enough,' her son said feelingly. 'Last week Mother sent them an apple pie. Mistress Henchley came into the kitchen just as I was about to give it to Mary. I had to pretend that Mary was giving it to me, and then Mistress Henchley lectured me for being greedy! It's a pity she isn't aware of other things,' Tom continued. 'Beth needs another gown, for instance. The ones she has are looking worn — and tight.'

'We may have some difficulty with that,' Lady Everard said. 'Lettice and Dorothy are both shorter and plumper than Beth, but if she appeared in a brand new gown even Mistress Henchley might notice and wonder where it came from. Last time Mary said she had found a forgotten parcel of cloth in a chest, but she can hardly do that again.'

'It's going to be a problem,' Tom brooded.

'Then distract yourself,' his father ordered. 'You can go and see how the corn is getting on. I'm hoping this year is going to be a good harvest.'

'He has always been very fond of Beth,' Tom's mother said musingly once he'd gone, 'but I don't think he regards her as a sister any longer.'

Her husband patted her hand.

'But I don't think Tom himself has realised that yet.'

He was thoughtful for some seconds, and then looked up at his wife.

'How would you feel if they did make a match of it eventually?'

Lady Everard smiled fondly at her husband and bent to kiss his head.

'Don't try to pretend to me that it's the first time the idea has entered your head. I think you've always hoped Beth and Tom would marry.'

'It would be a way of restoring poor Richard's family to the comfort and position they used to enjoy. And Beth would make him a wonderful wife, which is much more important. Unfortunately, Tom is still just a big brother to her, and she shows no sign of changing her opinion. I think she dreams of someone a little more romantic than our practical Tom.'

'I shouldn't worry about that too much,' his wife replied. 'She's only just eighteen. We can be patient.'

They might have been more worried about Beth if they had known what was happening at the little house as they talked.

Beth and Mary had hardly finished their work when there was a knock on the door. The old servant opened it to find herself facing a thick-set man in black with white linen bands at his neck and a high-crowned, felt hat.

The man stepped into the room without waiting for an invitation. Mary curtsied respectfully, though her face was set and cold, and a few seconds later, Beth gave a quick bob that showed much less respect. The man's small black eyes noted this.

'Do you not welcome a man of God, Mistress Elizabeth?'

Beth longed to tell him that he would

never be welcome, but she was conscious of Mary's warning look.

'A true man of God is always welcome,' was her ambiguous reply. 'I was surprised, however, that you should think it fitting to come to the back door, Minister Werham.'

Both of them knew that he had hoped to take them unawares and give him an excuse to find fault. His mouth tightened.

'Humility is a virtue we must all learn,' was his own double-edged answer.

Before she could reply, the door from the interior opened, and a woman dressed in deepest mourning entered. Eight years of sorrow had left Mistress Elizabeth Henchley thin and haggard, increasingly frail. Only her large dark eyes gave a hint of the former beauty which had attracted Richard Henchley at the court of Charles the First, the tragic king who had lost his own life under the executioner's axe in 1648.

She grew even paler, if possible,

when she saw the minister, and her hand rose to her thin throat. The Puritans had killed her husband and destroyed the familiar Church of England and the minister represented all she feared and hated.

'I felt compelled to call, ma'am,' he said to her formally, 'out of fear that some calamity might have befallen your household.'

'There has been no calamity, sir. What made you think so?'

'I could think of no other explanation why no-one from this house attended a church service yesterday.'

'My mother was not well,' Beth said hastily. 'Her head ached, so she stayed in bed and Mary and I nursed her.'

'You missed the Word of God for a headache?'

Mistress Henchley's eyes filled with tears, while Mary and Beth glared venomously at the minister. They knew the agonising headaches that the widow suffered, although they were both aware that they were always glad of an excuse to avoid Minister Werham's sermons.

'I trust your health will be better next Sunday, so that you may join with us in praying for the destruction of all enemies of our church and common-wealth.'

He waited for a reply, but there was no answer they could give safely, nor did he expect one, and he took his leave without another word. Mary and Beth were furious.

'Pray for the destruction of the rightful king, His Majesty Charles the Second, is what he means!' the servant spat out.

'Hush, Mary! He knows how we feel, but he can't trouble us if he never hears us say it,' Beth warned, vividly aware of Tom's timely instructions.

'I cannot go to church and pray for the destruction of the cause my husband died for!' Beth's mother said piteously. 'But if I don't go he will try to harm us! The man hates us because we are Royalists!'

'Everyone knows you are in poor

health, Mother,' Beth said soothingly. 'Forget Minister Werham. Sir Thomas will protect us.'

But Beth was uncomfortably aware of the trouble that a vindictive minister could cause, even to the Everards.

2

Beth slipped through the garden gate. It squeaked loudly if opened too far, and she did not want her mother to look out and see her on the way to Hatchford Manor where the Everards lived, even though it would probably take more than a squeaking gate to distract Mistress Henchley.

Beth had devoted the last two days since the minister's visit to soothing and reassuring her mother, but she was young, and confinement in the small house with the two older women grew wearying after a while.

Now she felt she had earned a brief respite, but although her mother reluctantly accepted the protection of the Everards, she still saw them as Puritans above all and frowned on any signs of the friendly relationship between her daughter and the neighbouring family.

Guided by the sound of voices, Beth found the ladies of the family assembled in the drawing-room, a stately apartment whose oak panelling contrasted with the elaborate white plasterwork of the ceiling. Mother and daughters were sitting by the window, using the light to help them sew.

She went to join them. Yards of fine, white cloth were spread around as they occupied themselves with embroidery of the linen. Lettice would take it with her when she was married in a few months' time to James Farnwell, the son of a landowner with farms adjacent to the Everards.

'Thank goodness you have come, Beth,' Lady Everard said after an affectionate greeting. 'I'm beginning to wonder if we shall ever finish this.'

'I don't think I could work on it, ma'am. You know I'm hopeless with anything except plain sewing.'

'But you could sort out our sewing boxes. I can't find anything I want.'

Beth started to sort threads and tidy needles.

Ever since Sir Thomas had brought them to Hatchford, the Everards had accepted Beth almost as a third daughter, and she was completely at ease with them. Sir Thomas and Lady Everard she loved, trusted and respected, and was always a welcome companion to their daughters. However, though she could relax and chatter with them, it was only with Tom that she felt free to discuss problems and air to him views that might have been unacceptable to the rest of his family.

They had been close ever since she had seen him standing at the door of his home waiting to welcome her mother and herself eight years ago. He had taken charge of Beth, and while the adults saw to Mistress Henchley, Tom had taken her daughter's hand and led her to the kitchen, where he made sure she was fed and given a seat by the fire.

Beth had been his faithful follower ever since. But recently a distance seemed to have grown between them. Tom seemed less ready to seek her out for friendly walks, just the two of them, and the other day had not been the first time when he seemed more anxious to tell her to curb her tongue than to listen to her. She wondered where he was today.

Lettice put down her needle and turned to her friend.

'Beth, have you heard that Mr Farnwell has promised to give us the dower house on his estate? You know Mr Farnwell's mother lived there for some years? It has been empty since the old lady died last year, and he has promised that it will be refurbished for us by the wedding!'

The bride-to-be was full of information about the size and number of rooms, the cupboards and closets of her future domain.

After an hour's work, the sewing group was broken up when Sir Thomas appeared, bringing with him not only his son but two other young men.

Beth curtsied as Sir Thomas came to greet her with a fatherly kiss.

'I'm glad to see you, Beth. You've been a stranger recently. You know James, of course?'

'Indeed I do,' she said, curtseying again to the tall, ruddy-faced young man with the dark brown cropped hair.

He was a frequent visitor and greeted Beth as an old friend. Tom, although he smiled at her, seemed a little abstracted and did not speak beyond a brief greeting.

It was the third young man who drew Beth's attention. He was tall, with black hair and hazel eyes, and his manner and dress showed an elegance unusual in rural areas. James introduced him as William Darnforth. His family estates lay a few miles on the other side of the Farnwells', and James had met him recently when Darnforth had returned from travelling in Europe.

When introductions had been made, the conversation became general, but it appeared that Beth had attracted

William Darnforth, for she found he had turned his chair so that they were a little apart from the others.

'Was it exciting to travel in Europe?' she said with naïve curiosity.

'It sometimes needed quick thinking and a steady nerve in these troubled times,' he responded, enjoying the artless admiration she showed.

Beth's secluded life meant that encounters with handsome, young men like William Darnforth were nearly non-existent, and she made a receptive audience for his accounts of his experiences.

'And what about you?' he said. 'I did not realise the Everards had such a charming neighbour. Do your family's lands lie near here?'

'I'm afraid my family no longer has lands.' Beth laughed at the idea. 'My mother and I live in the small house you passed near the gates. Sir Thomas was kind enough to give us shelter when my father was killed.'

'Did your father die following Sir

Thomas?' he enquired.

'Indeed no! My father died in the service of the king!' she replied proudly.

'I see,' Darnforth said, and soon after made a polite excuse and left her to join James and Tom.

She wondered why his apparent desire to get to know her had vanished so quickly and so completely. A little hurt, she occupied herself with tidying up the abandoned sewing.

Then the reason struck her. Of course, a man like William Darnforth, an eligible bachelor, a wealthy member of the country gentry, would want nothing to do with the poor daughter of a Stuart follower.

Beth stood deep in thought, conscious that her world was changing again. Lettice would soon be a married woman, and Tom was a man and growing away from her. Lettice's chatter made her realise how uncertain her own future was compared to the other girl's and how unlike Lettice's bright prospects it was likely to be.

She imagined a bleak, unending future in the cramped, little house, years spent looking after her mother and Mary as they grew old and infirm. Then what? A few years as companion, a type of unpaid servant, to one of the Everard girls, helping to care for their families?

Unknown to herself, Beth's face showed her unhappiness, and when Lettice and Dorothy went to give instructions for refreshments to be brought, Lady Everard took the opportunity to ask Beth quietly what was the matter.

'Is your mother ill again? Do you need something? You know you only have to ask, that we will do all we can to help you.'

'I was just thinking . . . that I will never be preparing for my own wedding.' Her voice wavered. 'No-one will want to marry me.'

Lady Everard took her hands comfortingly, while angrily wondering what young Darnforth had said to upset Beth.

'Nonsense, my love! You are a pretty and intelligent girl, and plenty of people will want to marry you.'

'Until they find out that Mother and I live on your charity!'

'Not every young man wants a large dowry. Some will appreciate worth.'

She remembered her recent conversation with her husband and decided to test the situation.

'Look at Tom. I'm sure he'll choose a wife for love, not money.'

Beth looked across to where Tom was discussing crop rotation.

'Tom? But he's so — practical. I can't imagine Tom marrying for love,' she continued. 'He's not at all romantic.'

'Romantic?' Lady Everard replied, a little put out. 'I'm talking about love and marriage, not romance.'

She looked at Beth's puzzled face, and broke into a laugh.

'I forgot, Beth. At eighteen, love and romance are the same, I suppose. But it is true love that brings lasting happiness.'

She looked at her husband, memories bringing a soft smile to her lips.

Lettice and Dorothy returned then, followed by servants bringing wine and cakes, and they all formed one group around the refreshments.

The peaceful atmosphere was broken abruptly. James had said something to Lettice which obviously distressed her, for her voice was suddenly raised in agitation. Everybody looked round.

'You don't mean that our marriage could be delayed if there is fighting?'

'Fighting?'

Lady Everard's voice was sharp with alarm. Like all women of her age, she dreaded a return of the bloodshed which the Civil War had brought.

'Charles Stuart,' her husband responded. 'He landed in Scotland from his exile in France over a year ago. Cromwell has already defeated one Royalist army and now he is driving the would-be king out of Scotland. He may gamble on bringing an army into England to claim his father's throne.'

'His own throne as he sees it,' James commented with a contemptuous laugh. 'Remember that farce of a coronation in Scone earlier this year?'

But Tom had seen Beth's pale, wide-eyed face.

'It's only a rumour,' he said firmly. 'If there is need for more action, General Cromwell and his army will deal with the Scots in their own country. Your plans won't be disturbed, Lettice. A little wine, Mother?'

By now the company had realised that the talk of war upset Lady Everard and Lettice, while the Royalist's daughter might not relish their comments on Charles Stuart, or Charles the Second, as he styled himself, and the conversation was awkwardly changed.

Soon afterwards, Beth murmured that Mary would be expecting her, and took her leave. Everyone said their good-byes with affection, with the exception of William Darnforth. He gave her a polite, small bow, but his eyes were cold. He was annoyed that

Farnwell had not warned him that the pretty girl was little more than a privileged servant. Beth was inwardly too excited by the news to care about his attitude, however.

She almost ran home and burst in on Mary noisily, seizing the old servant and dancing around the room.

'The king is coming! The king is coming! He's coming to claim his own!'

'Let me go while I've still got a breath in my body!' Mary commanded, disengaging herself. 'Now, sit down and tell me what you've heard!'

'King Charles is coming to England to claim his own at last!'

But when Beth had poured out her news, she was surprised to see the look of horror on Mary's face.

'Invading England with a Scottish army? Does he think that Englishmen will rise to serve him when he comes with an army of barbarians?'

'They are his subjects, as we are.'

'It was the Scots who surrendered Charles the First to Parliament. They sent him to his death on the block.'

Beth bit her lip and some of her excitement faded. She could not deny that in 1647 the Scots had sold Charles I to Parliament in exchange for the £400,000 in subsidies which England owed them. Once in Parliament's hands, his trial and execution had followed a year later.

'Don't let your mother hear a word of this!' Mary cautioned. 'She would think that the old days were coming back, and that will never happen. Even if the king were to regain his throne, England has changed for ever.'

It was a subdued Beth who went to her tiny bedroom that night. Mary's warnings had spoiled her joy at the news. Her only possible escape from a bleak future might be the triumphant return of the king. That could lead to the restoration of the Everards' property, and then young men like Darnforth could no longer look at her with disdain. But she remembered how her friends had reacted. Triumph for

Charles Stuart could mean tragedy for the kindly Everards and destroy Lettice's hopes for the future.

But gradually her thoughts became fixed on an image of the new young king, Charles the Second, twenty years old and fighting for the throne that was rightfully his after the martyrdom of his father on the scaffold at Westminster. A true figure of romance for a girl to dream about!

3

At first it had only been a rumour, speculation based on vague scraps of news, but suddenly it seemed that the whole countryside knew that Charles Stuart was coming to England with a Scots army at his back.

Lettice Everard was afraid only that the threat of war would disrupt her personal plans, and Beth found her in tears one day, convinced that her lover would be killed by the northern barbarians.

'There, there, Lettice,' Beth soothed her. 'It may all come to nothing. No one is sure that there is going to be any fighting.'

She tried to put her arm around Lettice, and was shocked when the young woman pushed her away angrily.

'You hope there will be war! You'd be glad to see us all ruined and Tom and

James dead if it meant that Charles Stuart could get his throne. Malignant!'

No Everard had ever used this Puritan epithet for Royalists to Beth before, and her ready temper flared. Instead of embracing Lettice she seized the shorter girl and shook her soundly.

'That is a wicked thing to say! You know your family is as dear to me as if it were my own . . . '

A cold voice broke in.

'May I know the reason for this interesting scene?'

It was Sir Thomas, attracted by the raised voices. The two girls separated immediately.

'Go to your room, Lettice. Compose yourself and bathe your eyes.'

Then he faced Beth, who confronted him with blazing eyes.

'What caused this to-do between you, Beth?' he demanded sternly.

'Your daughter called me a Malignant, and said I would be glad to see you all destroyed! It isn't true! I want the king to return, but you know I don't want you harmed!'

'I see,' Sir Thomas said quietly. 'Has anybody else called you names or treated you with disrespect?'

'Of course not!' Beth said, and then stopped.

Looking back over the past few days, hadn't people been unexpectedly cold towards her? Mistress Gambon and Widow Hampton, for example. She'd known them since she came to Hatchford, but when she'd seen them in the village street yesterday they had brushed past her without speaking.

'Well?' Sir Thomas said.

Beth sank into a chair, frowning.

'People have been polite — when I expected them to be friendly.'

'Beth, everybody is afraid of armies battling across England again. If Charles Stuart comes, then inevitably Englishmen will die. Like Lettice, the villagers are afraid for their sons and husbands. They are remembering that your father was an enemy who fought for the king.'

'And died for him! But I don't want

revenge. They can't see me as the enemy. Do you see me as a Malignant, your enemy?'

There was silence while Sir Thomas wondered how to continue. How could he explain the complicated web of interests and emotions to a young girl who still saw matters in terms of pure good and bad, as black or white?

'Beth, when the split between King Charles and his Parliament grew so great that it was past healing, most men, like me, thought it impossible that civil war should come to England. Then, when fighting did start, most of us believed it would soon end. But the war spread to the whole country, and I found that I had to make a choice. There was good and bad on both sides.

'I wanted England to remain a monarchy, but to me Charles was a bad and untrustworthy king who brought harm to England, and my view of religion and the proper government of the country inclined to that of Parliament. So I chose to oppose the king, and found myself fighting people like your father, who had been my friends.

'You know I do not think of you as an enemy, Beth. You are just as much a daughter to me as Lettice and Dorothy, but there are going to be difficult times ahead for you. Avoid the village as much as possible, and keep a still tongue in your head.

'Mistress Gambon's son was killed at Naseby, and Widow Hampton lost her husband at Marston Moor. If the situation grows bad, Mary and your mother, and you, must all come to stay here.'

'I thank you, Sir Thomas, but we will avoid that if possible. I don't know what it would do to my mother if she had to leave her home again, let alone the realisation that she might be in danger.'

She stood up, careful to hold herself with dignity, though inside she felt wretched. Sir Thomas also rose. Then a thought occurred to Beth.

'What if Minister Werham tries to hurt us? He is our enemy.'

'Leave him to me, Beth. He knows that I can make life difficult for him and that I would be glad of an excuse to have him removed from Hatchford.'

'Thank you, Sir Thomas. I am grateful to you.'

She turned to go, tears nearly spilling from her eyes, reluctant to let him see them. At that moment the door flew open and Lettice ran in, arms open.

'Beth, I'm sorry! I didn't mean it. I was just so worried about James!'

The girls embraced, and now Beth's tears were flowing freely.

'Of course I forgive you, Lettice. Come, we're friends again now.'

But in her heart a cold voice pointed out that for a few minutes even the girl who had been like a sister for eight years had seen her as an enemy.

When Beth passed Sir Thomas's advice on to Mary, the servant sniffed and commented that it was just commonsense.

'No-one's dared say anything to my face yet, but I've heard one or two comments made behind my back.'

By mutual agreement neither of them said anything to Mistress Henchley, who rarely left the house and was still unaware of events in the country.

But if Beth avoided going to the village, troublemakers could come to her. Beth was picking crab apples which grew in a hedgerow near her home, when she was surprised to hear a hated voice.

'Good morning, Mistress Henchley. I see you can't hide in your cottage all the time.'

Minister Werham stood on the foot-path between Beth and her home. His expression was one of sneering triumph.

'Not that hiding will be any use much longer. When the forces of God arise to crush Charles and his raggle-taggle army, even Sir Thomas Everard will not be able to protect Royalist sympathisers.'

Beth had disentangled herself from the hedge, and faced the minister with chin raised proudly.

'Will you please let me pass, sir.'

'You and your mother pretend to be ladies now, when you live on charity. Wait till your protector has gone, and you are begging from door to door for scraps. There'll be no Henchley pride then!'

Beth tried to push past him, but he seized her arm.

'You'll make a fine set of beggars — a useless girl, a broken-down, old servant, and a mad woman!'

Beth's self-restraint broke at this insult to her mother. She wrenched herself free of his grasp, bent down swiftly and yanked up some tall, stinging nettles that grew at the foot of the hedge. Using them as a whip, she slashed them time and again across Werham's face. He flung up his arms to protect his eyes, screaming shrilly like a woman, and Beth dodged past him and ran.

She glanced over her shoulder and saw Werham making for the village, and sobbed with relief.

Her hands were stinging badly from

the nettles now, and she hunted for some dock leaves to rub on them to soothe the pain.

Having done this, she made her way home and told Mary that she had fallen in a patch of nettles while reaching for some apples, and the pain had made her drop the bag of fruit in the hedge. The maid fussed over the nettle rash, while Beth assured her that it was getting better rapidly.

A few days later, Beth needed to visit a farm on the other side of the village. Somehow, probably through Mary, this became known at Hatchford Manor, and Tom appeared at the cottage door.

'Tom! Come in. Have you a message for us?'

'No message, but my father said you wished to visit the village, and I thought you might like me to escort you.'

She laughed up at him, but her eyes spoke her gratitude. She had been a little fearful of facing the villagers alone after her talk with Sir Thomas and her encounter with Werham.

'Are you to be my bodyguard? I shall be honoured, sir! I'll get my cloak.'

She whirled out of the room and Mary looked at Tom.

'You really think she needs guarding then, Master Tom?'

'I would have hoped that she would be safe in the village where everyone knows her, but I'm not sure. Minister Werham has been stirring up bad feeling against all with Royalist sympathies.'

'That man is a mischief maker without a Christian bone in his body,' Mary said furiously.

Beth felt relieved that Tom's tall figure was beside her during the half-mile walk to the village, though he was unusually silent. Previously, he would have strolled along, whistling casually, or joking and teasing her.

However, she was even more pleased to have him by her side when they reached the village. She was aware of people looking at her sometimes from windows or hastily-closed doors, but none of them greeted her as they would have done once.

Beth left the farmhouse a while later with relief, Tom lingering behind to pass on a message from his father to Farmer Woodley. Momentarily dazzled by the brilliant sun as she left the dark interior, she suddenly found herself face-to-face with Minister Werham. He unceremoniously pushed by her without a word, but before he could knock at the farmhouse door it opened, and the minister found his entry blocked by the tall figure of Tom Everard.

'Master Thomas Everard! Greetings!' The minister forced a smile.

'And greetings to you, Minister Werham. You do not seem to have seen Mistress Henchley.'

He muttered a greeting to her through gritted teeth and she nodded her acknowledgement, and then Tom took her arm through his and started to walk her back to her home without another word.

They were still on the outskirts of the village when they heard shrill screams coming from a small cottage set back a little from the road.

'It's Granny Walsh!' Beth exclaimed, instinctively turning towards the cottage, but Tom gripped her arm firmly.

'Stay here!' he commanded. 'I'll see what is happening!'

Beth stood still for a moment, but the screams grew in intensity, and she ran after Tom, eager to help the old woman. In the tiny back garden, the small figure of Granny Walsh was struggling in the grip of three young men whom Beth recognised as labourers' sons from the village.

The screams had covered the noise of Tom's approach, and he was on the youths before they realised he was there. His hefty fists laid two of them flat before they knew it, and the last released Granny Walsh hastily, who sank sobbing to the ground.

'Do you want to end in prison or the stocks for attacking an old woman?' Tom snapped, as the young men stood their ground.

'Prison? For doing God's work?' one of them questioned. 'She is a witch. Minister Werham said so, and we're going to throw her in the duck pond to see if she sinks or floats.'

'Listen to me, John Burman!' Tom stepped closer until he was face to face with the lout. 'If the minister is encouraging you to believe such superstitions, he will be in trouble as well as you. You might have killed her, and the penalty for murder is death by hanging!'

Granny Walsh clung to Beth who crouched by her protectively.

'They killed my cat,' she sobbed. 'Battered his head in with stones!'

'He was a devil, her familiar!' the young man claimed.

'Get home, all three of you,' Tom commanded in disgust. 'Remember, my father is a magistrate, and I know where you all live.'

The three slunk away, but when they were at a safe distance the spokesman turned round.

'Don't think your father can oppose

the work of God!' he shouted. 'How long do you think he will stay a magistrate when people hear that he protects witches as well as Malignants?'

'We've got to get help for Granny Walsh,' Beth said urgently.

The old woman was a huddled, sobbing bundle, but vivid bruises were beginning to discolour her wrists where the youths had held her.

'We'll take her to Farmer Woodley and his wife. They've looked after her before when she was sick.'

He picked the old woman up in his strong arms with little effort, and began to retrace his steps to the farm, Beth following.

As soon as Farmer Woodley saw their burden, he flung the door open and shouted to his wife. Soon Mistress Woodley was rubbing salve on the old woman's sore wrists while Beth stood by.

'There's no need for a fuss,' the victim quavered. 'Give me time to pull myself together, and I'll go home.'

'Not tonight,' Mistress Woodley said firmly. 'We'll see how you feel tomorrow.'

'Mary has a salve which is good for bruises,' Beth volunteered. 'I'll ask her to bring some.'

'No need,' the farmer's wife said without looking up. 'We can look after our own.'

Beth's face grew scarlet at the rebuff, as if she had been slapped.

Meanwhile, outside the house, Farmer Woodley was talking to Tom.

'She can't go back to her cottage,' he said heavily. 'Those young rogues will probably be back one night, and we can't keep a look-out all the time.'

'Then what's to be done?' Tom enquired.

'She can live here. She's some kin to my wife, and we've asked her to come here before, but she would cling to her independence. We may know she's a harmless, old woman, but there are plenty in the village who believe what

Werham says. Be careful, Master Tom. Don't give him a chance to attack your family. There's already enough muttering because of those you favour.'

He jerked his head significantly toward the farmhouse, and at that moment Beth came out the door with flushed cheeks.

'How is she?' Tom asked anxiously.

'In good hands. There's no need for us, so you can take me home.'

Beth told him how Granny Walsh wanted to go home, but Mistress Woodley was insisting she stayed.

'She'll never go home. She is going to live at the farm from now on,' Tom said briefly.

'Good! Then she'll be well cared for.'

'I'm not sure how she'll get on. Taken away from her home, her pet killed before her eyes by lads she knew as children. She'll just wither away.'

In Mary's welcoming kitchen, the courage which had enabled Beth to hold her head high during that walk left her, and she fell sobbing into the servant's arms while Tom explained what had happened.

'There, there, sweeting,' Mary soothed her. 'Sir Thomas will deal with the young fools and the minister. Now sit down, and I'll get a glass of wine for you, and I expect you could do with one as well, Master Tom.'

Rapidly she added hot water to some elderberry wine and added a pinch of spice. It was the comforting drink which she had used through the years when Beth had some ailment, and both the young people took it gratefully.

'From now on, Mistress Beth, I'll run any errands to the village until this fuss is over,' Mary said firmly. 'They may mutter as much as they like, but they'll think twice before they say anything to my face!'

'I think that would be a very good idea,' Tom said, but Beth shook her head vigorously.

'Why should I be forced to skulk at home? I'll be all right if you'll come with me, Tom.'

'Just think again, Mistress Beth!' Mary replied. 'If some hothead insults you, Master Tom will have to deal with him, and that will cause more ill-feeling. If someone says anything wrong to me, I'll just give them a tongue-lashing. Now you two finish your drinks while I see Mistress Henchley.'

'I don't see why everyone is against the king!' Beth said irritably. 'I know most people in this part of England are Puritans, but there must be some sympathisers who feel that England should welcome her true king!'

'No-one in England will welcome Charles Stuart while he comes with a Scottish army,' Tom responded heavily. 'He has entered England because Cromwell has conquered Scotland and driven him out, and now he is finding that even those who followed his father will not take up arms for a king who has bound himself to the Scottish Covenanters who betrayed that father. Charles himself betrayed Montrose, the best and loyalest Scottish soldier the Royalists had. Why should men fight for a man who allies himself with traitors and betrays his own friends? Charles Stuart isn't a conquering hero, Beth. He's a desperate man clutching at a last, feeble chance.'

Beth stood up with all the dignity she could muster.

'You are insulting my king, Master Everard.'

'Beth, I'm only speaking the truth!' Tom said, also standing.

Her face was set, and she did not reply. Indeed, she would have found it difficult to think of a reply. All she could do was be stubbornly faithful to her dream. Sir Thomas had said that people had to choose. She was making her choice. For all her short life her mother and Mary had instilled loyalty to the king in her. Now the villagers and her friends were rejecting her, already seeing her as an enemy.

Tom looked at her, and his own face grew stern. Carefully he put his glass down, and drew himself up to his full height.

'Goodbye, Beth,' he said sadly. He turned to go, and then suddenly turned back, seized her hand, and bent to kiss it.

Then he was gone, and Beth was left in a confusion of anger, surprise and sadness. His parting words had had a dreadful air of finality, and above all other feelings she was aware of a sense of loss.

4

Beth carefully avoided the village, but at the same time she felt reluctant to visit the Everards. She could no longer regard them just as her friends or feel that she was one of the family. Their loyalty was to Parliament and hers was to the King.

She was too full of energy to be a peaceful companion in the small house, and finally after one morning when she had been particularly restless Mary thrust a basket into her hands with instructions to go and pick blackberries from the hedgerows.

The peaceful pursuit of ripe fruit was very soothing, and she had half filled her basket when she was caught by a sudden shower. Looking round for shelter as the drops stung her face, she made for a small barn, the carefully-gathered berries scattering as she ran.

The door was unfastened and she stumbled inside, hoping she had not spilled too many berries.

The barn was scarcely more than a hut which Sir Thomas used for storage. She sank down on a soft pile of hay and listened as the rain drummed on the roof. It seemed to be settling into a regular downpour, and she stamped her feet on the floor in irritation, only realising too late that there were other things besides hay on the floor. Her shoe had come down in a pile of horse droppings. With an exclamation of disgust she stood up and brushed dried stalks from her dress, then seized a wisp of hay and began to wipe her foot.

Her eyes narrowed suddenly, and her hand stopped its work as she looked at the horse droppings with sudden interest. To the best of her knowledge, no-one had used the barn since the hay had been brought there earlier in the summer. Who had brought a horse into the barn? When had they been there?

She looked round with closer attention. Some of the hay had been piled up into a mound which could have been used as a bed.

It might have been a traveller who had decided to make use of the free shelter the barn provided when night had caught him on his journey.

She sat down on the 'bed' to ponder the question while the rain continued, and gasped as her hip hit something concealed in the hay. She rummaged in the hay to see what had hurt her. She felt something solid, and a quick scrabble revealed a pair of full saddlebags.

Obviously a traveller had stopped here, and the saddlebags indicated that he had probably come some distance. But he had wanted to conceal that fact and had abandoned his saddlebags and ridden off.

Who was the mysterious stranger? The secrecy indicated that he was up to no good. That could mean that he was a robber, spying out the land. She should warn Sir Thomas.

Beth drew in a sharp breath as she realised that wherever he was, he would have to return to the barn for his saddlebags.

Hurriedly she started to pile the hay back, then hesitated. The worn, nondescript saddlebags were under her hands. Perhaps their contents would give a clue about the horseman, more information for Sir Thomas to act on. Her fingers fumbled with the stiff buckles until the bags fell open, and the first things she saw were two pistols, placed so they could be quickly seized from the bags. This proved nothing. Any sensible man made sure he had some means of protection on a journey.

There were some shirts and breeches bundled together roughly. There was also a soft, leather pouch, and, as Beth picked it up, the neck opened and spilled out some coins which rolled on the floor. She rapidly picked them up to put them back in the pouch, and then her hands grew still as she saw that among the familiar copper and silver coins there were others.

She turned over some twopenny pieces, inspecting them carefully in the dim light. They had a two-leaved thistle on one side, and on the other side, a crown with the initials C.R. and the inscription CAR. D. G. SCOT. ANG. FR. ET HIB. R. 'Charles, by the Grace of God, King of Scotland,' she mentally translated the abbreviated Latin. And the thistle was the emblem of Scotland!

Here indeed were the clues she sought! Beth realised that she was holding Scottish money! Her fingers trembled with excitement as she pushed the coins back in the pouch and hid the saddlebags.

Although the rain was still falling, she wanted to escape before the owner of the saddlebags returned. She opened the door cautiously, picking up her basket first, so that she could slide out, closed the door behind her, and looked carefully around her. Then she gathered up her skirts and ran for the scanty shelter of the hedgerows. Catching her breath for a few seconds she then headed quickly for home.

Mary scolded her for getting wet and insisted on dosing her with a herbal concoction to prevent her catching a chill. Beth endured her fussing patiently, her mind still in a whirl of speculation. At supper even her mother noticed her abstraction and reproved her for her lack of attention.

But Beth was faced with a problem and had to decide what she should do. The unknown traveller was trying to conceal the fact that he had ridden here from some distance away. It seemed plain that this must be one of the Scotsmen who had come into England with the young King Charles, and almost certainly he had left the army to ride ahead and spy out the land and the sympathies of the people.

He was a hero, risking discovery and death to help the true king regain his throne! Beth had felt very jealous of this great adventure. If only a woman could be so daring!

That was when she began to wonder whether she, too, might contribute something to the enterprise. If the royal spy wanted information about sympathies and resources, where to find friends or enemies or food for the army, then she could give him that information and help her king!

She went to bed quietly that night, but lay awake until she had heard Mary attend her mother in her bedroom and then go to her own small garret where she slept on a truckle bed under the eaves. Beth forced herself to lie there for another half-hour. At first it seemed endless, but then she found her eyelids closing drowsily as she snuggled in the warmth of her bed.

She began to wonder if her plan was so wise. Perhaps she should stay here in safety. She sat up and told herself firmly not to be such a coward. Then she slipped out of bed and dressed herself hurriedly. She opened her casement window with great caution and peered out. It had been easy enough to tell herself that she would climb out of the window, but now the ground looked a long way away.

She looked round for help. If she put a chair under the window, she thought, she would be able to climb out and on to the roof of the porch, and from there she would be able to leap to the ground. Rapidly she threw her cloak out of the window and seized a chair.

The leap to the ground was a little more daunting than she had expected, and she landed heavily in an undignified heap, winding herself, and waited fearfully to see if there was any sound from inside the house. Luckily, she appeared to have roused no-one. Beth wrapped her dark cloak round her and set off for the barn.

Cautiously she retraced her earlier journey, hiding in the shadows of the hedgerow until she saw the black bulk of the barn. She crept nearer, and crouched behind a bush to observe the farm building. At first sight it seemed dark and silent, and she was ashamed of her sudden feeling of relief that now she could go home to the safety of her bed without any great deeds being required of her.

However, when she looked carefully, it seemed to her that she saw a dim light shining through the warped planks of the door. As she craned her neck to see better, she heard a horse whicker. The traveller had returned!

She was heedless of the wet ground, all her attention focused on the barn, when her heart seemed to stop suddenly and she felt very cold. The chill touch of metal had brushed her neck.

'Stand up and don't make a sound!' a harsh whisper came in her ear.

Scarcely able to control her legs, Beth rose. The pistol prodded her back.

'Into the barn!' was the command. 'Remember, if you try to escape or make a sound, my pistol is cocked and ready to blow your head off!'

She stumbled toward the barn, and the man behind her pushed the door open and thrust her in. Beth twisted round to see who had captured her. A dark lantern stood on a ledge, and by its limited light she saw a man's figure standing over her with a pistol aimed at her head. Even as she saw this, a hand reached out to pull her roughly to her feet.

'A woman?' he said in amazement. 'What in God's name are you doing out here?'

'I'm Beth Henchley,' she explained, hating the quaver in her voice which betrayed her fear. 'I am for King Charles, like you, and when I realised that you were hiding here I thought I could come and give you information which might help.'

'What makes you think I follow Charles?'

'The coins, the Scottish coins in your purse.'

'So it was you who came here today. I saw things had been moved, so I was expecting a visitor. I was waiting outside, and you were easy to hear, alerting every animal for a mile. But I didn't realise the spy was a woman.'

He looked her over leisurely, and she felt her face flush hotly at the casually insolent manner in which his gaze lingered on her face and body.

'Suppose I do follow the king?' he said, putting down his pistol. 'What have you got to offer?'

'I can tell you who opposes him in this part of the county,' she stammered. 'And I know who has stores that his army might need.'

'Is that all? I learned all I needed in a few hours in a Worcester inn,' he said. 'Can't you offer more? No gold, no jewels or silver plate?'

She shook her head dumbly, hating him for shattering her dream of aiding the king. The way he was surveying her made her uncomfortable, and she began to feel scared as well as humiliated.

She tried to back away from him, but

found herself trapped against the wall. Now he came even closer and seized her chin in one hand, tilting up her face so that he could examine it better.

'Perhaps you brought me something worth having, anyway,' he said musingly. 'Something to comfort a soldier facing battle soon.'

And now his body was pressed against hers, and as he bent to kiss her, one hand seized the neck of her dress and ripped it. She tried to twist her face away and scream, and felt laughter shake him even as he pulled her ever closer.

'Scream if you like. Who's going to hear you?'

In panic she managed to free one hand and tore at his eyes, narrowly missing but scoring his cheek with bloody lines.

He swore, and exerted his strength to throw her down on the makeshift straw bed. For a split second she was free to take a deep breath and let it out in a piercing scream, but then his heavy body was on her and she was helpless against him. Through her fear, she was dimly aware of the sound of the hinges squealing as the door was thrust roughly open. She heard another voice.

'Who's here? What's going on?'

As her attacker scrambled up, Beth sat up, clutching her torn dress to her. The newcomer saw her and gave a shocked cry.

'Beth!'

It was Tom, with a large bag in one hand and a stout stick in the other.

The stranger launched himself at Tom, who dropped the bag, side-stepped and tripped him with his stick, but the man was instantly on his feet again, reaching for his pistol. Desperately Beth threw herself over it.

The man kicked her in the side, but the momentary delay gave Tom his opportunity, and there was the solid sound of his stick meeting bone as he struck the man's skull. The stranger collapsed on the hay while his panic-stricken horse reared.

'Have you killed him?' Beth kneeled, clutching her dress round her.

'Not yet,' Tom said, feeling the pulse in the man's neck. 'But he'll stay quiet for some time. Beth, what are you doing here? Did he — hurt you?'

She shook her head dumbly, and then reached out blindly for the comfort of his familiar figure. She burst into desperate sobs, clinging to him.

'He — he tore my dress. I came to help him but he attacked me, and then you came!'

'What did you expect?' Tom said, shocking her into silence. 'You come to meet an unknown soldier in the middle of the night. Did you expect some polished, polite gentleman?'

She bent her head in shame, realising how naïve she had been, and hurt by his evident contempt.

'What do we do now?'

He looked down grimly at the unconscious figure.

'We go home.'

'And him?'

'We leave him where he is. He'll have come to in a few minutes, and then he'll ride off as soon as he's able.'

'But you can't just let him go after what he did to me!'

'What do you want me to do? Take him back to my father to stand trial? Are you prepared to let everyone know what a fool you've been?'

He stood up abruptly and handed Beth her cloak.

'Wrap this round you. The best thing we can do is get you home and try to keep this secret between us.'

He bent to pick up the pistol, and then ushered her out. She felt almost too weak to walk, and clung to his arm as they started back. She was grateful to him for saving her and yet aware of resentment at the way he seemed to be judging her. She felt she had to justify herself to him.

'Maybe I was impulsive and foolish, but if you were me, spending day after day in the same dull routine, you would have seized the chance to do something! You may be happy with your cosy, little world of hay and apples, but I want more. I was trying to help the king against his enemies!'

'And who were these enemies?' Tom asked. 'My parents? My sisters? Me? The people who have sheltered and helped you and your mother? You came here to give a stranger information which would help him destroy us?'

She dropped his arm and they walked on in silence. When they came to the banks of a stream he drew the captured pistol from his pocket and weighed it in his hand. Then the moon caught a flash of metal as he hurled the weapon into the water. He stood still, not looking at her.

'Would you have been happy if a ball from that pistol had killed me?'

'Of course not!'

'Why not? A Royalist bullet killing a Puritan?'

They continued on their way. Tears ran down Beth's cheeks. The combat of divided loyalties was ready to break her heart, but faced with the reality of a threat to the Everards, the figure of the king seemed very shadowy.

To fail in her allegiance would be denying everything that her father had died for and her mother had taught her to believe, but the sordid episode back in the barn had stripped the glamour from the king's cause for her.

She was conscious of relief as they neared the cottage. She wanted the warmth and security of the bed she had foolishly left, and felt almost too tired to stand. When they reached her home, however, she looked up helplessly at the open window of her bedroom.

'How did you plan to get back in?' Tom asked curtly.

'I can climb through my window from the porch top.'

'And how will you get up on the porch?'

'I got down easily enough!'

But when she was actually standing by the porch, she realised that it had been much easier to leap down than it would be to climb up.

'Step on these, as if you were stepping into a stirrup,' Tom commanded, linking his hands together.

She did as he said, and he lifted her into the air so that she could reach the porch door by an undignified scramble. From there she was able to tumble head first into her bedroom.

When she stood upright and put her head out of the window to thank Tom, he had already disappeared.

5

In spite of her exhaustion, a turmoil of emotions kept Beth awake for some time after she had stripped off her ruined dress and thrust it into a corner of a cupboard. She would have to think of some story to tell Mary about its condition, but that would have to wait.

When she arose after a few hours of sleep, she was so pale and heavy-eyed that her mother remembered how quiet she had been the previous evening and decided she must be sickening for something.

But Mary knew the kind of emotional upset that young girls were prone to, and quietly wondered what had gone wrong between her nursling and Master Tom to make him avoid their house. Mistress Henchley was still unconcerned.

'If you are not well, Mary will have to

take a message to the Manor.'

'Why should the Everards need to know how I feel?'

'Have you forgotten that Sir John Farnwell and his lady are to be guests at the Manor today? Lady Everard requested me to let you be one of the party. Of course, I cannot be pleased that you will be a guest of those who oppose the king, but you are young, and Mary seems to think that you should be enjoying gatherings with other young folk.'

Beth was touched by her mother's rare concern for her, unaware of how hard Mary had worked to persuade her mother that Beth should be allowed to accept the formal invitation which Lady Everard had sent.

She saw it as an opportunity to thank Tom for last night, and possibly explain to him her good resolutions for the future. She could not bear to think of them remaining on bad terms. She rose and kissed her mother fondly, wincing a little at the pain of her bruises and was very glad that none of them was visible.

'Don't fret yourself about me, Mother. I shall enjoy the visit.'

But in fact she found herself feeling very unhappy indeed later at the Manor. It was not the fault of the entertainment. Lady Everard had done her best to make this a special occasion.

Expensive French wines had replaced the usual home-made elderberry and cowslip wine, and all manner of delicacies had been produced which Beth would usually have greeted with a healthy appetite. Sir John Farnwell and Lady Farnwell and their son were not to blame. Beth had met them all several times, and was quite at ease with their friendly, down-to-earth manners.

But it was some time since she had met their daughter, Clarissa Farnwell. That young lady had spent most of the previous two years in London, where she had stayed with an aunt who had introduced her to London society.

Clarissa soon made it clear that although the good burghers of London were now godly people, free of the tyranny of a monarchy, their style of living and entertainment was still far above that of rural Worcestershire. She let it be known, several times, that she had met many of the members of the aristocracy who had sided with Parliament.

The older people listened with good-natured amusement to her stories, though Lettice and Dorothy were open-mouthed with awe and eager to learn all they could about city life, while James Farnwell treated her with the lofty tolerance of an elder brother.

It was Tom's behaviour which upset Beth. He seemed to be fascinated by the newcomer, staying attentively by her side and listening to all her gossip as though he were deeply interested in the latest fashions. Beth could not understand it. Surely he could see how silly the girl was!

She inspected her narrowly, almost certain that Clarissa's blonde hair must have received some assistance to have formed such ringlets. Surely it had been virtually straight before she went to London? And that narrow waist must have been achieved by very constrictive lacing to make such a contrast with the ample curves of bust and hip.

She was also painfully aware of the difference between Clarissa's gown of dark blue silk, trimmed with lace and ribbons, and her own simple dress of black cloth, limp from much wear.

Sir Thomas was not too busy acting as host to the Farnwells to miss Beth's frown, and though he was sorry the girl was not enjoying herself, he wondered hopefully if she was feeling a touch of jealousy.

Lady Everard was very content. The evening had gone well and Lady Farnwell was an old acquaintance who had flattered her by asking for the recipe for candied rose petals.

Tom seemed very taken with Clarissa Farnwell, and although she knew her husband's hopes about Beth, Clarissa would be a good match for her son, binding the two estates closely together with two marriages.

At the moment Clarissa seemed to show regrettably too much preoccupation with dress and society, but she would soon settle down after marriage to a sensible husband. Anyway, Beth had shown that she did not view Tom as a possible husband for herself.

Beth felt very isolated. Everyone was sharing in the enjoyment except her. The rest of the young people had formed a cheerful group around Clarissa, while parents discussed more sober matters separately. Beth sat quietly withdrawn in the window seat of a large bay, wondering how soon she could politely make an excuse and go home.

She was tired after her adventure the previous night, and was developing a bad headache. She was angry with herself for caring so much about Tom's behaviour. If he preferred to court a stupid, boastful girl, she could save her thanks for another time.

Brooding savagely, she was taken by

surprise when she heard Tom's voice beside her.

'I brought you this, Beth. My father thinks highly of it. What is your opinion?'

He held out a glass of wine, glowing red in one of the crystal goblets that were only brought out on special occasions. Beth accepted it with almost inaudible thanks, and was surprised as Tom took a seat beside her.

She was not to know that Tom had avoided her so far, not because he was angry with her, but because he also was still shaken by his feelings of the previous night. The thought of what the man could have done to Beth made him feel sick to his stomach and when he'd realised she'd been in such obvious danger the depths of his feelings for her had become glaringly apparent to him.

Dismayed, he had realised that he would never again be able to think of Beth as the playmate and companion she had been for the past eight years.

Now she was a woman who stirred in him feelings he had never known before. He felt he had been robbed of the past, and did not yet know what to do in the future.

The two sat side by side, sipping the wine. It was one of Sir Thomas's best, and they made polite comments about it while still preoccupied with their thoughts about each other. Then Beth scolded herself for her rudeness. She owed her life to Tom. Beth summoned up her courage to make her carefully-prepared speech of thanks.

With eyes fixed firmly ahead, she began, 'I want to thank you, Tom, with all my heart, for what you did last night . . . '

'For what? For my rudeness? I behaved unforgivably towards you.'

'Whatever you said was justified!' Beth turned towards him, amazed.

'No, Beth.' He shook his head. 'What you did, you did because of your brave heart, your faithfulness to what you believe in. It isn't your fault if others cannot live up to your standards. I am sure that brute was not typical of the many brave gentlemen who follow Charles Stuart.'

Sudden colour stained her cheeks. The previous misery of the past hours was forgotten as she savoured this gracious tribute. Then she remembered something which had been puzzling her all day.

'It was fortunate for me because you could come to my rescue, but what were you doing out in the fields at that time of night?'

'You have to promise you'll never tell anyone.' He hesitated, a wry grin spreading over his face. 'I was out poaching rabbits.'

'Poaching?' Her voice rose with incredulity, and he hushed her rapidly.

'Your father owns the estate! Why should you poach your own rabbits?'

'Well, perhaps poaching is too extreme a word, though some of the rabbits did belong to the Farnwells.'

He looked guiltily at her as she

waited for further explanations, torn between amusement and surprise.

'You accused me of liking my quiet routine. Did it never occur to you, Beth, that at times I, too, might grow tired of my quiet life and long for excitement and adventure? Just occasionally, I like to be alone under the stars, free from all my duties and away from my family.'

'At least, I can guess now where Granny Walsh's rabbits came from!' A mischievous smile dimpled Beth's cheeks. 'It's just a little difficult to imagine you as an elf or fairy. Where are your wings, Tom?'

Tension broke as they laughed together. He found he had taken her hands in his and was looking down at her enchanting face with all the happy friendship which he thought had gone for ever.

Then, with her warm hands grasped in his, Tom Everard had a revelation which was to change his whole life. Beth was a beautiful and desirable woman, but she was still, at the same time, his friend and companion.

He did not have to choose one aspect or the other. Beth combined both in one marvellous whole. He realised that he loved her in every possible way and wanted her for himself for ever. He wanted to marry her.

'What's the matter? You look as though you had just had a very important idea,' Beth queried.

He looked at her with amazement. Couldn't she tell from his face what was on his mind? No, he realised sadly. He knew now that he loved her and wanted to marry her, but to Beth he was still Tom, the almost-brother, no figure of romance or desire.

'I have, Beth.' He patted her hand gently. 'Probably the greatest idea of my life, and some day I will tell you about it, I promise you. Meanwhile, let's go and see what the others are doing.'

His parents noted with approval how he had drawn Beth back into the main party, little dreaming that their son was wondering desperately how he could transform himself in Beth's eyes from brother to lover.

* ⋆ ⋆ ⋆ *

The beginning of September saw the sad touch of autumn on the Worcestershire countryside round Hatchford, but Beth's spirits still had something of the light-heartedness of summer. Tom was once again her friend, calling at the little house nearly every day with messages from the Manor or bearing small gifts from his mother to be discreetly smuggled into the house in case Mistress Henchley should see them.

Beth's gratitude was reinforced by her gladness that her oldest friend had overcome the coldness that had fallen between them. It was Mary who saw the new note of respect and admiration that the young man showed.

She wished Tom and Beth well, but could not help remembering how differing Richard Henchley's courtship of her mistress had been. She recalled the love tokens of jewels and flowers and sonnets, the long summer afternoons of polite flirtation as the ladies and gentlemen of the court strolled through the flower gardens. A leg of lamb and an offer to weed the vegetables was so much less romantic!

Then even this prosaic courtship was threatened when Clarissa Farnwell made her move. Her first priority after her reluctant return from the gaiety of London was to ensure a future where she would be maintained in the comfort to which she had become accustomed.

After visiting several of the local families, she decided that although plain Tom Everard would make a very dull husband, Tom Everard as heir to the extensive Everard estates was a very desirable match.

She began to accompany her brother when he visited Lettice. Once there, she attached herself to Tom very firmly. When he went to the stables, Clarissa insisted on going, too. When he wanted to check whether the apples were ripe for picking, she accompanied him and praised the yield as if he were personally responsible for the rain and sun that had nourished and ripened them.

But her admiration seemed to have no effect, and with a sharper eye than her brother for such matters, she suspected that Beth might be the reason why Tom seemed able to resist her charms. Well, the charity brat would have to be dealt with.

'Tom, I promised Mary some duck feathers for pillows,' Lady Everard mentioned one afternoon when Clarissa was present. 'Will you take them over? If I send a servant,' she explained to Clarissa, 'Mistress Henchley wants to know why, but she accepts Tom's visits as Beth's friend.'

'Why not go now?' Clarissa exclaimed. 'Let me come with you, Tom. I have always wanted to see inside that dear, little house.'

Half an hour later, they set off. Tom clutched a billowing bag of feathers under his left arm, while Clarissa hung possessively on his right, keeping close to him so that her expensive perfume could not be missed.

Beth and Mary had not been expecting visitors and were busy preserving fruit. Steamy pans bubbled on the fire, and Beth's dark hair was straggling across her heat-flushed face. She was dressed in an old gown covered with a fruit-stained apron, and certainly did not welcome a visit from the fashionably-dressed Miss Farnwell.

'How provident!' Clarissa exclaimed, peering at the preserves. 'How convenient!' she commented on the tiny parlour.

Fortunately for her, Mistress Henchley was resting in her bedroom, otherwise her impertinence would have been sharply rebuked.

Finally Clarissa could find nothing more to pry into without going farther beyond the bounds of good manners, and she and Tom took their leave.

Once out of the house, Clarissa shook her head and sighed sadly.

'Poor girl! What kind of future can she hope for?'

'She can rely on the Everards to help her,' Tom said stiffly.

'Charity? What a pity there is nothing else for her.'

Suddenly she turned to Tom as if an idea had just occurred to her.

'But of course! I've had a wonderful idea! My Aunt Frances in London needs a nurserymaid. A well-mannered girl like poor Beth is just what she wants, and that old woman could stay and look after her mother here. Once in London she may well meet with some respectable shopkeeper or steward who would be willing to overlook her parents. I'll write to my aunt at once.'

'You'll do no such thing!'

Tom's anger drove him beyond politeness, and Clarissa gaped at him.

'I mean,' he said, controlling himself, 'that my father considers himself bound to keep her under his personal protection. He would never let her go.'

'How silly!' Clarissa pouted. 'But I'll try to think of something else.'

'There is no need,' Tom said firmly. 'Beth is our responsibility.'

He peered closely at Clarissa with an alarmed expression.

'Is that a spider on your neck?'

As Clarissa screamed, gathered up her skirts and ran for the house, Tom smiled grimly to himself. It served Clarissa right — if she hadn't been such a busybody, there'd have been no need for him to scare her a little.

After that incident, Clarissa's visits to Hatchford grew fewer, and Beth and Tom resumed their old relationship.

But there were some matters that Beth and Tom avoided discussing. Word had reached the village that Charles Stuart and the Scots were drawing nearer, then that they were less than fifty miles away, and finally that they had occupied Worcester in late August, but both Tom and Beth carefully refrained from mentioning the topic.

It was an obstacle that might part them for ever, but Tom's principles were as deeply ingrained as Beth's. He could not abandon what he believed in, even for her. It was for this reason that he sought an interview with his father in early September.

Sir Thomas looked up from his accounts in enquiry as the tall figure of his son entered his study, and he laid down his pen.

'Some problem with the farm, Tom?'

Tom shook his head, but stood silent and indecisive.

'What is troubling you, then?'

Tom took a deep breath, and looked at his father levelly.

'I came to tell you that I feel it is my duty to volunteer to fight with the forces of Parliament against Charles Stuart.'

'Are you serious?' Sir Thomas jerked upright abruptly.

His son began to respond, but Sir Thomas waved him to silence.

'Forgive me, Tom. I realise that you are indeed serious. But why?'

'Charles Stuart has led a wild rabble of Scots into England, and as a gentleman of England I feel I should be ready to defend my country.'

He stopped and looked down at his father. Would he understand his desire to take action against the invaders? After all, he had been a fighter himself in the past.

'Sit down, Tom,' Sir Thomas instructed quietly. 'I respect you for your resolution, but I feel there is no need at present for you to join the Parliamentary forces.'

He held up a warning hand as Tom opened his mouth to speak.

'Let me finish. I have thought about this, because I had wondered whether I should take up arms again myself, in spite of my grey hairs. But the conduct of war has changed considerably since the late king and Parliament first fought each other.

'Then any man could ride to join the

army of his choice, and a brave heart was all that was demanded. But generals have learned that untrained troops can be worse than useless, however brave. Nowadays victory goes to disciplined, experienced troops, and we have General Cromwell on our side and his New Model Army.

'They have beaten Charles Stuart out of Scotland, and will beat his Scotsmen in England when they catch them. By bringing the Scots into England, Charles Stuart has alienated even his English well-wishers. The Scots will be defeated. They have some fine fighters, but they lack organisation. Cromwell will crush them easily.'

'You mean I would be a nuisance to this trained army,' Tom said bitterly.

'Possibly. At the most, they could make little use of you. Stay at home, Tom. You are needed more here. If the Scots reach Hatchford, you and I will have our fill of fighting.'

He paused, then added, 'If you go, you risk breaking your mother's heart, and I would never rest happy till you returned safe and well. Besides, there is another matter I did not intend to speak to you about yet. I doubt if Beth Henchley could ever forgive you if you actually fought against the man she sees as king.'

He noticed how Tom's head lifted at the mention of Beth's name. His son chewed his lip thoughtfully.

'I suppose you are right.' He sighed. 'I was being foolish, imagining myself riding gallantly into battle, fighting gloriously, as you did. Well, such heroics are not for me. I'll get back to my cows and dream no more.'

He half-rose, but his father said sharply, 'Sit down!'

Surprised, Tom did as he was bid. His father faced him earnestly.

'Never think of war and battle as glorious, Tom. Yes, I fought at Newbury. I saw good men cut down, dead or maimed in an instant, leaving widows and children to mourn and suffer. I was pitifully afraid, and I killed others simply to prevent them killing me. And when it was over I found my friend, Richard Henchley, dying.'

'And for eight years you have sheltered his wife and daughter, as he begged you to . . . '

'Begged me? He was dying in agony with a sword thrust through his guts. He did not even know that I was there, and I was glad when death stopped his screams. There was no touching death scene with the separated friends reunited at the end.'

'You mean you lied to Mistress Henchley?'

'What was I to do? Tell her that her beloved Richard died writhing in pain, clutching his guts into his belly? I brought back a lock of his hair and said that he had sent it. I lied to spare her and to give her a reason to let me help her, but every day of my life I remember how my friend really died. There is no glory in war!'

His breast was heaving as he fought for self-control, and his face showed sick disgust at his memories.

'Now you know that I lied, and have maintained that lie for eight years. Will God forgive the sin?' Thomas Everard bowed his head.

'I think God will see it as a very Christian deed. Don't worry, Father. I'll stay. Instead of destroying my fellow men, I will help to feed them.'

He left quietly, but the accounts lay untouched before his father for some time. Sir Thomas Everard was brooding on the question that had haunted him for eight years. In the bloody confusion of the battle at Newark, could it have been his sword which fatally wounded Richard Henchley?

6

September the fourth was a glorious day. The splendour of warmth and colour outside helped Beth when she persuaded Mistress Henchley to take a rare outing and accompany her and Dorothy Everard on a walk to harvest the fruits of the hedgerows. Mistress Henchley approved of Dorothy. She thought the girl showed a proper respect to a Henchley, even though her father was now a well-respected magistrate.

They had wandered from field to field at random, moving farther from home than Beth had realised, until her mother sank down on a stile, fanning her delicate face with a sprig of leaves.

'Enough, Beth. I'm growing weary. Let us make our way back now.'

Looking round, her daughter realised with some dismay that the quickest way back to the cottage would take them through the village. She remembered the possible hostility from the villagers to those known to support the Stuarts and she hesitated.

But it would only take them five minutes to pass through the centre and she was sure that the villagers would show their usual courtesy and under-standing to her mother. There would be a risk, but she saw how fragile her mother looked in the clear autumn sunlight.

She sat upright, but her hands lay limp in her lap, and the twig of leaves had slipped to the ground as though she found it too much effort to hold them. They would have to take the short cut through the village.

'Take my arm, Mother, and we'll soon be home with our harvest.'

'I'll run home across the fields,' Dorothy volunteered. 'I'll see if Tom can come and meet you.'

Mother and daughter made for the road, the village already in sight. Beth saw no-one in the first few houses they passed, and her hopes rose that they might avoid any awkward confrontations. Perhaps every able-bodied villager was out helping with the harvest or gleaning on this fine day.

Then, as the road curved gently to bring them in sight of the little village green, she halted abruptly. There were all the villagers, it seemed, gathered round the figure of Minister Werham who stood head and shoulders above the other figures, apparently standing on a box or chair so that he could be seen and heard by everyone.

'We'll have to go back, Mother,' Beth whispered, 'and take the long road round. That man always means trouble for us.'

But it was too late. There was a yell, and Minister Werham's hand was pointed at them in triumphant denunciation.

'Look!' he shouted. 'Malignants who would have rejoiced to see your sons and husbands killed by the invaders, your women attacked by the savage

Scots! Now their fellow-traitors lie dead at Worcester, and Charles Stuart's head will soon be off his shoulders!'

'Quick Mother!' Beth urged. 'As fast as you can!'

It was too late. The villagers had turned and surged towards them, led by the preacher, and soon surrounded their prey.

Beth faced them bravely with chin held high, while Mistress Henchley stood silent and bewildered. Desperately, Beth sought for allies. She saw familiar faces in the mob and appealed to them.

'William Cobbold! John Smithers! Help us, or there will be trouble when Sir Thomas hears about this!'

But all she got in return were threatening looks and fists shaken at her.

Suddenly the crowd parted as Werham pushed through and stood face to face with Beth. She realised that he was also drunk, with triumph as well as ale. He stood red-faced and rocking on his feet, sneering at her.

'The proud Henchleys! Beggars who live on the misguided charity of a man who has shown too much friendship to Malignants!'

He turned, raising his voice, and addressed the crowd.

'Why should they escape their just punishment?'

There were shouts of approval, though Beth saw with relief that some, more sober than the others, were beginning to look anxious and quietly withdrawn as things seemed to be getting out of hand. But Werham still had many eager supporters, including the strangers, and no-one was actually coming forward to defend the two women.

'Why should the evil-doers live?'

Now the villagers were abandoning him more urgently, eager to escape involvement in any violence, but there were some shouts of agreement. Suddenly stones started to whistle through the air, and one hit Beth on the shoulder, making her gasp with pain

101

and let go of her mother's arm.

Mistress Henchley stood alone for a second, and then a large stone, flung with brute force from the back of the crowd, struck her on the forehead, and she fell to the ground, blood steaming from her head.

Desperately, Beth flung herself across her mother's body to protect her.

'Murderers!' she screamed at the crowd.

There was a chaotic scene as the men close enough to see what had happened tried to break away while others tried to press closer to the Henchleys. Beth turned from them, reckless of her own safety, and crouched by her mother's body, cradling her head in her lap. Mistress Henchley's face was chalk-white, her eyes were closed, and there was no sign of life.

Tears streaming down her face, Beth felt for a heartbeat, failed to find one, and tried to control her shaking hands as she made another attempt.

Suddenly there was the pounding of

feet as a tall figure raced across the green to Beth's side, thrusting through the villagers. Tom kneeled beside her, his face strained with alarm as he looked at Mistress Henchley.

'What happened? Dorothy said you were walking home . . . '

'Till Minister Werham urged a drunken crowd to kill us!' Beth spat out.

The minister was one of the few who had not fled. The conviction of his righteousness and the false courage of drink still emboldened him, though he took a step backwards as Tom stood up and faced him.

'God has struck down the army of Charles Stuart,' he proclaimed, 'and all his followers shall suffer likewise. Rank and noble blood are to be swept away in the New Jerusalem!'

'So, Master Werham, you are a Leveller as well as a murderer!' a new voice said from behind him.

Sir Thomas Everard stood there, ice-cold fury in his face.

Werham checked in his tirade and swallowed what he was about to say. Even in his present state, he knew that Sir Thomas Everard, magistrate, would take ruthless action against a man who had urged the murder of the Henchleys. Rapidly he swung away across the green in the direction of his house.

A few villagers stood a safe distance away, curiosity keeping them there to see the end of the drama. Sir Thomas beckoned two men imperiously.

'Samuel Bourne and John Torrance! Take the shutter off the inn window and bring it here! Robert Crouchley — run to the Manor as fast as you can and tell my wife what you fools have done!'

He gazed angrily around, memorising the guilty faces.

'I shall remember you, and you will pay for this. I'll have no cowardly women-killers as my tenants!'

Tom meanwhile had pressed his fingers under Mistress Henchley's jaw.

'I can feel a pulse,' he reassured Beth,

and hope lit up her face.

He did not tell her how weak the faint flutter of life had been.

The shutter had been wrenched from the inn, in spite of the publican's protest, and Tom and his father lifted mistress Henchley gently on to it, covering her still form with their coats. The two men who had fetched the shutter carried the makeshift litter with its burden toward the Manor.

Beth walked beside it with her mother's cold, unresponsive hand clasped in the youthful warmth of her own, and Tom strode along near her, his eyes on Beth as much as on the wounded woman. Sir Thomas followed, leaving the villagers to sober up and reflect on what the future might hold.

Robert Crouchley had taken his message to the Manor, and had then gone on to tell Mary what had happened to her mistress. The sad, little procession saw her running towards them, tears steaming down her face.

'What have they done to you, my

darling?' she wailed. 'Haven't you been hurt enough?'

When they reached the Manor, Lady Everard was already waiting, ready to take charge. Soon Mistress Henchley was in a bed hastily aired with a warming-pan full of coals from the kitchen fire. Lady Everard gently bathed the blood from her face and examined the ugly wound carefully.

'Head wounds always bleed generously,' she reassured Mary and Beth. 'I can find no sign that the skull itself is broken, but it was a bad blow. All we can do is bandage her head, keep her warm and wait.'

'If only I hadn't taken her through the village! This is all my fault!' Beth said in abject misery.

'Nonsense!' Lady Everard said robustly. 'The fault belongs with the louts who threw stones, not with you.'

She put her arms around the girl, and realised Beth was shaking.

'What a fool I am! You have been through an ordeal as well. Come with me and I'll give you a cordial to soothe you. Come and warm yourself by the parlour fire. Mary will sit with your mother.'

She was well aware that nothing would have moved Mary from her mistress's side. So Beth was cosseted and comforted, and left in the care of Lettice while Lady Everard went in search of her husband who was with Tom in his study. Her reply to their anxious enquiries was not encouraging.

'I don't know what will be the outcome. It was a heavy blow. Mistress Henchley may recover consciousness in a while, or she may sink deeper into a coma and die. You know she has had no great will to live since her husband was killed. What have you found out about this to-do?'

'We've got some information from the men,' her husband responded. 'Apparently Werham told the truth when he said that there had been a battle at Worcester yesterday. Cromwell's Ironsides finally caught up with Charles

Stuart yesterday outside Worcester. Some say that three thousand Royalists died, and thousands more are prisoners. Charles Stuart fought bravely, but is now a fugitive with every Parliamentarian soldier searching for him.'

'That was the reason for Werham's behaviour. War is threatening again.'

'I doubt if we will be affected. It seems that Worcester is probably Charles Stuart's first and last battle. It's said that some of the rabble that follow the Ironsides brought the news — rascals who had been preying on the dead on the battlefield, so had money for drink in their pockets.'

'What will you do about Werham?'

'He's given me the opportunity I wanted. He was urging riot and murder, so the law can take action against him. His friends won't dare defend him when they hear about his Leveller talk.

'Cromwell knows as well as anyone that talk of the abolition of rank could lead to the collapse of order in the country. It was one of Parliament's greatest fears that all social order might collapse when the monarchy was removed. Werham has no future now in Hatchford, and he knows it.'

'Someone said that he was seen stealing away from the village soon after we rescued Mistress Henchley and Beth,' Tom added.

'It seems that it was the strangers who were responsible for the violence,' Sir Thomas remarked. 'Our villagers were willing enough to drink when someone else was paying, but they say that was all they did.'

'They are all claiming that it was the strangers who were responsible for the stone-throwing and threats,' Tom said.

'That may be true, but I'll let them stew for a bit,' his father stated.

While Sir Thomas interrogated the servants in case any more information could be gleaned from them, vigil was maintained in the sickroom by Beth and Mary. Lady Everard wisely let Beth return to this duty as soon as she felt fit enough, knowing that it would make her feel that she was of some use.

The invalid was still unconscious when evening came, and the Everards took great care to secure the house and outbuildings in case any of the strangers should come prowling around.

An hour before midnight, the stableman on guard became aware of a flickering red light in the sky, then a crackling sound. Standing on a mounting block, he peered over the stableyard wall, and what he saw sent him hammering at the door of the Manor.

'Fire! Fire! Mistress Henchley's house is afire!'

Tom, who had not yet gone to bed, was one of the first to reach the scene. The thatch of Beth's home was blazing, fiery sparks leaping along the roof, and it was obvious that the roof timbers were already alight as well.

'Hooks! Get hooks to pull off the burning thatch!' Tom shouted as the menservants appeared one by one. But

Sir Thomas, coming up just in time to hear this command, shook his head.

'Too late,' he said. 'The fire's got too strong a hold.'

Servants started to fill buckets of water with the vague idea of dousing the flames, but there were too few of them to affect the progress of the fire and they soon gave up the attempt. Tom tightened his first in helpless fury.

'But how did it happen?' he demanded. 'There was no fire in the house. Mary had the kitchen fire put out for safety's sake.'

'This fire was started from the outside, deliberately,' was the grim answer. His father pointed. 'Look how the thatch is burning from the upper layers. If there was no fire in the house, it couldn't have been a spark from the chimney which started the blaze. This is arson.'

Father and son watched impotently as the fire spread. Then Tom turned abruptly as he heard a wail, and saw Beth running toward the cottage. He stepped in front of her and stopped her from going towards the house.

'Stay away, Beth! There's nothing anyone can do. The fire's got too good a hold.'

The red gold of the flames lit up her desperate face.

'Everything we had — clothes, the few things Mother had saved . . . '

Her brown eyes widened and her mouth fell open in horror.

'What's the matter?'

'Tom! Father's portrait!'

He, too, remembered the picture which was Mistress Henchley's pride. It showed Richard Henchley in all his youthful splendour. Now that record of the dead man, and the skill of the painter, would soon be no more than a handful of ashes. He looked at the burning house, then sadly shook his head.

'It's too dangerous, Beth. Look at it. Nothing can stop the fire now, and the heat is almost too much to bear here.'

She tried to tug herself free from his

grasp, weeping with frustration as his strength held her still.

'But it will kill Mother if she loses his picture! It's in the parlour and the flames haven't reached there yet. Let me go. I could get it in seconds!'

Tom still held her firmly as he tightened his lips and looked at the burning house measuringly. Then he nodded decisively to himself. Before anybody could guess his intention, he had thrust Beth into Sir Thomas's arms and plunged towards the burning house, where he thrust the door open with his powerful shoulders and disappeared through the gaping black hole. Smoke started to billow through the opening.

As servants yelled and pointed, Beth stopped struggling, and she and Sir Thomas stood transfixed. Nothing could be seen beyond the door.

It seemed like an hour but could only have been a couple of minutes before they could see signs of movement and then a figure loomed through the smoke. Tom reappeared in the doorway and lurched into the fresh air. A few yards from the building he stopped, swaying and coughing.

In his arms he held a large object protected by a curtain torn hastily from a window. Two grooms ran to him and one took the portrait of Sir Richard while the other seized him by the arm and hurried him away from the flames to safety.

He sank down helplessly near his father, gasping air into his smoke-filled lungs. His hair was singed by the flames and his face was black with soot.

Beth hurled herself down beside him, and he turned toward her, but instead of pouring out gratitude she beat him with his fists.

'You fool! You idiot, Tom Everard!'

Taken unawares, Tom reeled at the unexpected onslaught.

'Enough!' he gasped. 'You wanted the picture so much that you were willing to risk your life. I got it for you!'

'By being reckless and stupid! Why

should you risk your life for our picture? How could I have faced your family if any harm had come to you? You were stupid, stupid!'

'You ungrateful wretch! If that's all the thanks I get, I'll pitch it back in the flames!' he said, bewildered and furious as he struggled to his feet.

'Don't you dare touch it! And here is my thanks!'

With the same passion she had shown when she attacked him, she threw her arms round him and kissed his smoke-stained face soundly. Thoroughly confused, he held her to him and patted her back, not really sure what to do.

'You'll get soot on your dress, Beth. These clothes are ruined.'

'What does that matter?'

Sir Thomas echoed her reaction as he grinned at his son in relief.

'Who cares about a few clothes? She's right, you were a reckless fool, but you got the picture and survived. Now take Beth back to your mother, while I get this mess under control.'

Even as he spoke, there was a great crash as the blazing roof gave way and collapsed into the body of the house, sending showers of painful sparks over the onlookers. Everybody ran for safety.

'Get back to your mother, Tom!' Sir Thomas ordered again. 'By now some fool will have told her what you did. Beth, see his burns are salved.'

Tom and Beth hastily made for the shelter of Hatchford Manor, where his mother seized him, cleaned him, and tended him.

Left to supervise the scene, Sir Thomas wondered if Beth had realised yet that the sooty dress she was wearing was the only one she had left in the world. What would happen to the Henchleys now?

7

The next day brought no comfort. Blackened walls and fallen timbers were all that remained of Beth's home for the past eight years. Nothing had been rescued from the smoking ashes except the picture of her father, which was now propped up in the room where her mother lay, ready to console her when she recovered consciousness.

She showed no signs of doing this, her pale face still and silent on the linen pillowcase. During the night Beth had dozed off in the armchair where she sat by her mother, but Mary had stayed awake, grimly watching over the woman she had cared for as girl, wife and widow.

In the grey light of dawn, Mary was bending over her mistress when Beth saw her hesitate, shake her head, and suddenly clutch at the bed as if she were about to fall. Beth hurried to support her to a chair.

'You're not well, Mary. I'll call Lady Everard.'

'No! I'll not leave your mother!'

'You'll be no use if you collapse! Go and lie down on the bed next door. You know I'll call you if you are wanted.'

'Perhaps I could do with a rest.' Mary hesitated, then nodded reluctantly. 'I keep forgetting I'm not so young as I used to be.'

She climbed heavily to her feet and started slowly towards the door, pausing by the bedside to look down at the still figure.

'I thought she would be safe at Hatchford, that Sir Thomas and I could look after her.'

'You've kept her safe for years, but it seems nowhere is entirely safe from this war,' Beth responded. 'Let me look after her now, Mary. You've earned a rest.'

She sat patiently by the silent bed. It seemed ironic that she had worried about the Civil War bringing danger to the Everards, but had never thought that she and her mother might be in peril.

It occurred to her that this was probably the longest she had ever spent alone with her mother. When her mother was not in her bedroom Mary was usually present, and when her mother had been ill in the past it had been Mary who had nursed her.

The hours dragged by and still Beth's mother did not stir. Lady Everard came in frequently to check on the condition of the invalid and her two nurses. She searched her stores for delicacies to tempt their appetites, and with gentle firmness she persuaded them to eat some of the food she had sent to them, but there was little else she could do until there was some sign of change, for better or worse.

Frustrated, she went to see her husband and asked him challengingly what he intended to do about Minister

Werham and his trouble-making follow-ers. If Werham had given him legitimate grounds for complaint he should take action against him.

'I am trying to, my love. Unfortu-nately the rogue seems to have vanished. I sent a servant to demand that Werham come to the Manor and account for his behaviour, but the servant found the house empty. I think Werham has realised how bleak his future would be in the district and has fled the village during the night.'

'The villagers are still swearing that they did nothing, and they were badly shocked by the wanton destruction of Mistress Henchley's home,' Tom com-mented, newly returned from a visit to the village.

'They did nothing to help Beth and Mistress Henchley either,' his father said grimly. 'In a few days I may accept their apologies, but I'll warn them about their future behaviour if they want to stay as my tenants.'

It was early evening before Beth saw

any difference in her mother. Then she noticed her head move very slightly on the pillow. Immediately Beth was on her feet, bending over the bed and beckoning to Mary. Her mother became restless and tried to lift a weak hand to her injured head. Seconds later, her dark lashes fluttered and parted, and she looked up at the three anxious faces vaguely and then with apparent bewilderment.

Lady Everard slipped a supporting arm round her, and with Beth's help lifted Mistress Henchley so that Mary could hold a cup to her mouth and persuade her to drink a few mouthfuls of cordial. The invalid still looked confused, clearly wondering where she was.

'You hurt your head,' Lady Everard said gently, 'so we brought you here to Hatchford Manor to be nursed.'

The patient gave a trace of a grateful smile, and lay quiet against the arms of her friend and daughter, her eyes wandering round the room. Then her gaze found the portrait of her husband and became fixed on it.

'We thought the portrait would comfort you, so we brought that as well,' Lady Everard added.

The sick woman nodded feebly, and her lips parted. All she could manage was a whisper, and they had to strain to hear what she was saying.

'Please, make sure that my husband knows where I am when he returns,' the three women heard her murmur, and then she closed her dark eyes and Mistress Henchley sank back into sleep.

'She's not herself yet,' Lady Everard said urgently, as she saw Beth's horrified face. 'Wait till she stirs again.'

Beth relaxed a little, reassured by this statement, but the older women looked at each other with foreboding. There had been no sign of recognition in Mistress Henchley's eyes when she had looked at her three nurses.

She did not stir again until near dawn. Her pulse seemed a little stronger, but once again she looked at her daughter and life-time servant as if she had never seen them before. Her eyes fastened eagerly on the portrait, and she asked if her husband had returned yet.

'Not yet, madam,' Mary responded with stiff lips.

'Wake me as soon as he comes.' And she returned again to deep sleep.

Further periods of consciousness brought no change, Mistress Henchley, strangely calm and incurious about her wounded head, was eager only for news of her husband, and failed to recognise her servant or daughter.

Lady Everard had persuaded Beth to take some rest and change her clothes for some of Lettice's. Tom saw her as she came wearily down the stairs and his heart twisted with love and misery.

Her head was bowed as if too heavy for her slender neck, and there were dark shadows under her eyes. The worry of the past two days seemed to have thinned her face and emphasised the beauty of her bone structure, and she had a new maturity.

She smiled shyly at him, and hesitated on the last few stairs.

'I haven't seen you to thank you for what you did yesterday,' she said. 'But then you always seem to be rescuing me.'

'I'm only sorry I came too late to save your mother. I understand there is little change so far.'

'I'm afraid not.' Beth's shoulders sagged. Then she saw the white bandages half-hidden by the big cuffs of his coat. 'Oh, Tom! I didn't know you'd burned your poor hands!'

'Just a few blisters which are almost better,' he assured her, 'but the bandages will give me an excuse to have a rest from harvesting.'

She tried to smile at the poor joke.

'What do you want now, Beth? Can I help you?'

'It's sounds funny but I feel a little bit hungry — do you think I could have some bread and fruit?'

He escorted her into the parlour to a

comfortable armchair, and then rang for a servant.

'Bread and soup for the lady,' he requested when the maid appeared. 'And something light to appeal to her appetite. And some wine.'

Beth lay in the great chair, content to relax with closed eyes and silently aware of Tom's comforting presence until a little noise and bustle announced that the food had arrived. Tom poured her a glass of wine and ladled out some soup. She was so exhausted that the spoon trembled as she took her first mouthful.

In spite of his bandaged hands, Tom took the spoon gently from her and fed her like a child until the warm broth gave her some energy and she insisted she could feed herself.

'Has that made you feel better?' Tom enquired when she'd finished.

'I feel much better bodily but has Lady Everard told you about my mother? It nearly broke Mary's heart when she didn't recognise her.'

He nodded sympathetically.

'How about you?'

'It's different for me. Mary has known her since she was a child, but my mother and I have never been close, especially during these past eight years. Now it looks as if I will never know her better.'

'It's early days yet, Beth. Give her time to recover.'

Beth bit her lip, staring into the depths of the fire on the hearth. Then she looked directly at Tom.

'It sounds dreadful, I know, but will it be a good thing if she recovers? She was unhappy enough before, but now we are destitute. We haven't even a change of clothes. The few belongings we had are all gone. The souvenirs of her life in the past — the apostle spoons, miniatures of her family — they were all destroyed.

'How do you think she will feel when she realises that? You know how she has managed to avoid facing the fact that we depend on you for almost everything. In your house she will have to acknowledge that we are living on your charity. Her pride and dignity will be gone.'

'You know we don't regard it as charity. You are part of our family . . . '

She went on as if he had not spoken.

'It would have been better for her if she had died when the stone struck her. Perhaps even now she will just fall asleep and never wake up, die thinking that her husband is coming home to her.'

'Can you really wish your mother dead?'

'It would be kinder than reality. As it is, she may well recover physically but not mentally. She may never recognise me again as her daughter. The trouble is,' she went on wretchedly, 'that while my heart should be breaking for her I keep thinking of myself. I am eighteen. Even if your father will give us shelter, for how long must I care for a madwoman? What future would I have after her death? I will not be the first woman, I know, to have been born a lady and die a servant, because that is what I will be, even if your mother calls me a companion or guest. And I don't think I can face it!'

Tom placed one bandaged hand on her shoulder, and her heart swelled with gratitude for his understanding.

'Oh, Tom! If only you knew what a relief it is to be able to speak frankly to you, my one true friend!'

Before he could respond another thought struck her.

'And I can never go back to the village or face the villagers again!' she said passionately. 'People I thought were my friends, whom I've known ever since we came here, turned into drunken louts who threatened my mother and me!'

'Weak heads and too much ale,' Tom said soothingly. 'They're already very sorry for what happened, and will do all they can to make amends.'

'They can do nothing!' She swung round furiously. 'I never want to see them again!'

'Don't fear the future, Beth. This is not the time, but I have plans . . . '

Tom broke off, mentally cursing, as his mother entered in search of Beth.

'You've rested and eaten?' she enquired, wondering why her son was looking so blackly at her. 'Then if you will go back to your mother, I'll see that Mary has rest and food now.'

She bore Beth away upstairs, but soon afterwards Tom found an opportunity to tell his parents of his conversation with Beth.

'She's too clear-sighted,' his father commented. 'I hoped that nursing her mother would occupy her mind fully for the time being so that she had no chance to fret about the future.'

His mother reflected for a while before she spoke.

'The trouble is, there is little for her to do for her mother,' Lady Everard said. 'With Beth and Mary, as well as the maids and me, we're tripping over each other to look after a woman for whom we can do very little except keep her clean and warm. But what else can she do?'

'She can visit my Aunt Elizabeth at Moseley!' Sir Thomas suddenly announced to his startled son and wife.

'Aunt Elizabeth?' Tom queried in amazement. 'But she's in her eighties! And what grounds have you got for sending Beth there?'

'As you say, the old lady is in her eighties. As a dutiful nephew, I should enquire whether the disturbances have upset her. And as Dorothy has certainly been upset by what has happened here, I shall send her to her great-aunt for a little comforting, and I shall send Beth with her.'

'Isn't Moseley rather near Worcester?' Tom commented doubtfully.

'It's south of Worcester, and any Royalist fugitives will be going north, striving to get back to Scotland. Although if they did head south, they would find plenty of friendly sympathisers. Beth will find more fellow-Royalists there than she does in this area.'

'But you can't send two young girls there out of the blue,' Lady Everard expostulated. 'It will upset the old lady.'

'So long as I send a servant in advance with a couple of hours' warning, she and her household will cope without any trouble. My aunt may not always be sure whether it is now the reign of Elizabeth, James or Charles, and I'm sure she hasn't grasped the idea of a Commonwealth.

'But as far as daily life is concerned she is still very alert, and every time she writes to me she complains that I don't send our children to see her often enough. A visit from two young girls with stories of drunken mobs and vanishing ministers will delight her.'

From his infrequent encounters with the lady, Tom recalled a tiny figure who used language associated with the robust style of Good Queen Bess, enquired into all his doings with embarrassing frankness, and who never hesitated to thwack him with her stick when she wanted his attention.

'If anyone could take Beth's mind off her troubles, then Great-Aunt Elizabeth can. I find her fascinating but exhausting whenever you send me there. Do you want me to escort them?'

'I'd like you here in case Werham and his friends reappear with any more mischief in mind,' his father said. 'Richard and James can escort them there, and you can ride over with any news in a few days.'

'Beth may not want to leave her mother,' Lady Everard warned.

'Leave it to my powers of persuasion,' her husband said confidently.

He sought an interview with Beth within the hour. As Lady Everard had predicted, she protested at the idea of abandoning her mother to the care of others, and at first refused point-blank.

But Sir Thomas persisted, telling her that Dorothy would need her company and reassurance on the journey and in the presence of her aged aunt. He also touched on his concern about Werham, giving her to understand without actually saying so that he was afraid for her safety, and that it would be one worry fewer for him if she were safely elsewhere.

He also hinted at the additional responsibility she was for Lady Everard, and at the undoubted fact that his wife and Mary were both better and more experienced nurses than Beth.

It was a masterly performance, and finally Beth agreed to go, but not until she had sought out Lady Everard and been told that any major change in her mother's condition would be unlikely for some time.

'Tom will ride over and keep you informed of everything, anyway.'

So Dorothy was told that recent events had upset her more than she knew, information that confused her until she realised that it would mean a visit to her Great Aunt Elizabeth. A makeshift wardrobe was hastily assembled for Beth and all other necessities found for her.

While the women scoured their

wardrobes for petticoats and stock-
ings, Tom made his way to the sad
remains of Beth's home. There was
still a little daylight left. Perhaps he
could find among the ruins something
which had defied the flames, which
Beth could take with her as a
keepsake.

The blackened walls still stood head
high, but the windows gaped emptily
and the little garden had been trampled
out of existence. Soon villagers would
take the unburned timber for their fires
and re-use the stone from the walls to
create new buildings. Within a year all
trace of the house would probably have
vanished.

The ashes had cooled, and he poked
among the rubble with a stick held
gingerly in his sore hands, but could see
nothing worth saving.

The stone chimney stack still stood,
and he wandered round it, head bent.
Neither he nor the man coming in the
opposite direction saw each other until
they collided. Tom started to apologise

automatically, and then realised that the other man was Werham!

His clothes were creased and soiled, his white linen collar discoloured with soil and soot, his hair matted. The smug expression had gone as well. When he saw Tom he glared like a wild animal, his mouth working.

'Minister Werham! My father has had men looking for you.'

'Do you think I am going to come to him like a schoolboy, to be chided and then sent away in disgrace? No! I have done with Hatchford. But before I go, Master Thomas Everard, I will take my revenge on your family.'

His right hand came out of his coat pocket clutching a large knife, and he advanced towards Tom.

'I have been watching for a chance to harm your father. How do you think he will feel when he finds that his only son is dead?'

Tom cursed his clumsy bandaged hands. The only thing he could do was run for his life, but even as he glanced behind him another man appeared with a musket in his hands. His escape was blocked.

'Choose between the gun and the knife, Thomas Everard,' Werham jeered. 'My friend has no liking for magistrates or their sons either.'

Suddenly there was a shout from nearby. Two men approaching the ruined house had seen the weapons and they broke into a run. Cursing, Werham rushed at Tom, who threw himself aside, only to trip and fall full-length on the ground. As he did so, he heard the deafening sound of the musket behind him, and there was an agonised scream.

When he scrambled painfully to his feet he saw Werham lying on the ground, and one of the newcomers in hot pursuit of the musketeer. Tom had fallen on his injured hands, and for a moment he closed his eyes, giddy with pain. Farmer Woodley was kneeling by the minister's body when he looked again, and had opened his coat to reveal a bloody wound.

'He was trying to kill me!' The events of the past few minutes had happened so rapidly that they seemed unreal.

'I know,' the farmer replied. 'He took the shot aimed at you, however. My brother and I saw it all.'

His brother returned, panting. The killer had outdistanced him.

They looked down at the body of the man who had been respected and powerful among the villagers. Now he was dead, killed while he attempted murder himself.

'I'll bring my cart,' Farmer Woodley said. 'We'll lay him out in his own bed.'

'No-one will believe that he tried to kill you,' his brother marvelled.

'There is no reason for anybody to know that,' Tom said sharply. 'Let the man keep some honour. Say that a robber killed him when he disturbed him near our house, and leave it at that.'

Farmer Woodley and his brother looked at each other, and nodded.

'It's better than he deserves, but it

will tidy things up without too much fuss,' Woodley said. 'Leave it to us. You know we can keep silence.'

Tom went to tell his father that one threat had gone for ever.

Early on the morning of the seventh of September, while horses were being led from the stables and prepared for the journey, Beth went to take her leave of her mother.

She stood by the quiet bed and looked at her mother's face. Relaxed in sleep, she seemed to have grown younger.

'That's how she looked when your father was alive,' Mary said quietly.

Beth kissed the unresponsive face on the pillow and turned to her old servant and friend.

'Am I doing wrong to go, Mary?'

'No, my love. What there is to do here, I can do better than you.'

'But suppose she were to die, and I wasn't here?'

'She said goodbye to us and everyone eight years ago when your father died.

The last years have only been a living death for her.'

Beth and Mary embraced each other, then the young girl left Mary to continue her vigil.

Down in the courtyard, everything was ready for the journey. Two grooms, heavily armed and watchful, were to escort them and another had already gone ahead to inform Mistress Everard of her approaching guests. Dorothy was full of excitement, and her mother had to remind her quietly that she was supposed to be suffering from shock.

Even Beth felt a stirring of anticipation. This would be by far her longest journey in eight years. She was young and strong, eager for experience. Tom noticed the sparkle in her eyes as he helped her up into the saddle, and smiled up at her.

'Don't let Great-Aunt Elizabeth frighten you!'

'If she does, I'll send for you to come and save me.'

'Send for me whenever you need

help. You know I'll come.'

Their eyes met and there was a sudden moment of awareness and realisation between the two of them that went unnoticed by others amid the noisy bustle as Lady Everard checked that nothing had been forgotten.

Then the grooms led the way out of the courtyard to start the journey and the girls' horses followed. Beth craned round and saw the tall figure of Tom standing with his eyes still fixed on her. He waved one bandaged hand at her, and turned away abruptly.

8

For the first few miles of the journey Beth rode along automatically, her horse placidly following the stable companions ridden by the two grooms. Dorothy was too busy talking to the grooms about what towns and villages they would pass through to notice her silence.

The young girl would have been appalled if she had guessed that Beth's main wish was to abandon the expedition and return to Hatchford Manor. In spite of Sir Thomas's eloquent persuasion, Beth still felt that she should have remained with her mother. In addition, she wanted to see Tom, to discover what his last words to her had really meant.

They made good time, for Sir Thomas wanted them safe in his aunt's house that night, not exposed to risks in a country inn when the area was still in a turmoil after the battle at Worcester.

They were reminded of this when they rounded a bend in a lane and found themselves confronting a small band of armed riders. The grooms' hands flew to their pistol butts, Dorothy gave a little scream, and the blood drained from Beth's face as the horses came to a sudden halt. Then Richard and James relaxed as they recognised the buff, leather coats and lobsterpot helmets as the uniform of Cromwell's troops.

'No need to worry,' Richard said quietly to the two girls. 'These are our men, not Royalists.' But Beth's heart was still racing.

The leading figure, obviously the officer in charge, barked an order, and his troops reined their horses to a standstill as he rode forward to interrogate the group. Richard hastily dragged out the travel permits which Sir Thomas had supplied and explained where they were going.

'Unwise at this time,' the officer observed. 'What do you think your two pistols could do against a party of Charles Stuart's Scotsmen?'

'Sir Thomas said we wouldn't meet any round here, that they'd all be making for the north,' Richard said anxiously.

'He guessed wrong, a typical civilian's mistake.' The officer gave a bark of contemptuous laughter. 'Our soldiers are barring the way home to Scotland for the Malignant troops, so many of them are heading south, trying to make for London or the Channel ports. But we're rounding them up steadily. There'll be very few who escape.'

'Charles himself? Has he been taken?' Beth risked a question.

'Not yet, madam.' The officer shook his head. 'There was a rumour he had been. He left Worcester when he saw the battle was lost, and was riding with a group of Cavaliers. Most of them have been captured and it was thought at first that he was among them, but we've heard now that he left his comrades before our lads caught up with them.

'But don't worry about him, ladies. We'll have him soon, and then he'll quickly have his head off his shoulders, just like his father.'

The officer thrust the travel papers back into Richard's hand, and saluted the two girls as he and his troops rode past to scour the fields for fugitives.

Later in the day, Beth and the rest of the party saw a dozen soldiers who had been successful in the hunt for Royalists. They rode along proudly, followed by an equal number of prisoners whose wrists had been tried together with ropes which were fastened to their captors' saddles.

As they watched, one man collapsed with a groan, but the soldier leading him rode on, dragging the unconscious man along the road's dusty surface.

Beth gave an indignant cry of horror, but before she could say or do anything Richard's hand was on her reins.

'Leave it,' he said quietly. 'There's

nothing we can do.'

'But he's killing the poor man!' she said in a furious whisper.

'Perhaps the poor wretch would prefer to die now rather than live to be hanged,' Richard replied, still holding her reins.

They looked at each other for a long moment. Apart from other matters, they both knew that it would be risky to draw attention to herself. A few questions in the Hatchford locality would reveal where her sympathies lay. She nodded slowly. He released her reins, and they rode on.

Eager to escape from both the patrols of soldiers and possible Royalist fugitives, the two grooms hurried the horses along. Beth and Dorothy, unused to such a long day in the saddle, were now tired and looking forward to the end of their journey. Dorothy was becoming increasingly irritable.

'We must have missed our road,' she complained. 'We should have reached my great-aunt's house before now.'

Beth reminded herself that the younger girl was little more than a child, and set herself to soothe her companion with reassurances about a speedy and safe end to their journey.

She was relieved, however, when James, peering through the thickening dusk, announced that he could see the lights of Millfeld House ahead. Soon their horses clattered into the courtyard of a red-brick mansion, and James went to announce their arrival while Richard helped the girls dismount.

They felt stiff, clumsy and cold, but the door opened speedily when James knocked. Those in Millfeld House had obviously been ready for their arrival, and soon a groom had appeared to show Richard and James where they could stable their horses.

The girls mounted the short flight of stairs to the door and were received and ushered into the warmth of the entrance hall by an elderly butler who assured them that the lady of the house was eagerly expecting them.

Dazzled by the light from the wax candles that filled the sconces, Beth and Dorothy were gazing shyly around at the handsome, oak furniture when a door was flung open and a small figure advanced to welcome them with open arms. Sir Thomas had warned the girls that his aunt had not adapted completely to Puritan England.

The lady was just over five feet tall in her high-heeled shoes, and in spite of being nearly eighty years old she was dressed in full-skirted scarlet satin, with several ropes of jewels around her neck. For her age she had a surprisingly dark head of hair, and Beth suspected that she was following the example of the great Queen Elizabeth and wearing a wig.

Beth, accustomed to the Puritanical good taste of the Everard household, stared at the vision with fascination. Even Dorothy, who had seen her before, was dazzled. She hurried forward, and greeted each of them in turn with a smacking kiss.

'I've been expecting you for these two hours or more! Meg will take you to your room to refresh yourselves, and then we will have supper in the small parlour. I want all the news!'

Meg was a smiling, elderly maid who took them up to the comfortable bedchamber they were to share. Hot water and linen towels were waiting there, and the maid helped them to unpack a few clothes and change. Within thirty minutes they were seated by a warm fire where Meg served them with a generous supper, not forgetting a glass of mulled wine to warm them after their journey.

Mistress Elizabeth Everard hovered over them like a butterfly, urging them to take another glass of wine or some more spice cake. They were indeed hungry, having only eaten some cold food packed up for them by Lady Everard, and they made a hearty meal. Aunt Elizabeth, as she insisted the girls should call her, smiled with satisfaction.

'My cook is delighted to have a chance to cook for someone with a good appetite. She complains I eat like a bird, and don't give her a chance to show off her skills properly.' She took her seat close to the girls as Meg cleared away the remains of the food. 'Now, tell me everything.'

Sir Thomas had kept his elderly relative informed of matters affecting his family, such as Lettice's engagement to James Farnwell, but she was eager to learn all the details about the forthcoming marriage. Beth tried to answer Aunt Elizabeth's questions, as Dorothy began to yawn and struggle to keep her eyes open, but the sharp-eyed hostess saw what was happening.

'Forgive me! I was forgetting what a long journey you've had! I must keep some questions till tomorrow, when you have had time to rest.'

She pulled the bell to summon Meg. While they waited for the servant, she turned casually to Beth.

'If Lettice is getting married, isn't it

time Tom did so? Has he a sweetheart yet?'

Beth thought of her former fears about Clarissa Farnwell, and then of Tom's parting words to herself.

'I think he finds one young lady very attractive, but nothing has been said,' she responded briefly.

Aunt Elizabeth gave her a glance that seemed to perceive a lot, and Beth blushed hotly, glad of the diversion caused by Meg's appearance.

'Good-night to the pair of you,' Mistress Elizabeth said. 'It's a long time since two such pretty girls have stayed here. No need to worry about gallants hiding under the bed, though. You're safe here!'

It was pleasant to rise the next morning and find themselves the centre of eager attention. Aunt Elizabeth's servants were enjoying the novelty of two young guests as much as their mistress. Richard and James had left early together with the servant who had gone on before them to announce that they would be coming.

Beth enjoyed the comfort and attention, but could not forget what they had seen the previous day. At the back of her mind was always the question of whether her king, Charles Stuart, was finding a way to escape from his enemies or was already a prisoner.

Aunt Elizabeth had learned something of Beth's background and what had happened from Dorothy, and came fussing to comfort her guest, wearing a gown of green velvet lavishly trimmed with fur.

'I may be Sir Thomas Everard's aunt,' she began, 'but I've spent most of my life under the rule of a monarch, and though neither James nor the first Charles were worthy of comparison with Elizabeth, I preferred them to the jumped-up set of squires and soldiers who claim to rule us now. So do most people around here.

'It's not like Hatchford. I can name you a dozen gentlemen with Royalist sympathies round here. Thomas Whit-greave, for instance, at Moseley Hall. He's suspected of being an active Catholic, as well as a Royalist. If any fugitives turned up at his door he'd probably help them, whether it was a common soldier or the king himself.'

'Moseley Hall?'

'You passed it last night about a mile from here. It's a house with three gables and stands by the road.'

'Yes — just after we passed four men who didn't want us to see them clearly.' Beth's eyes widened. 'Perhaps they were fugitives!'

Mistress Everard nodded briskly.

'Then they will have got some help and comfort there. So stop worrying your pretty, little head about matters you can't help, and come and tell me about this house that Lettice is going to move into.'

But Aunt Elizabeth had domestic matters to see to before she could settle down to more family gossip, and suggested that the two girls should explore the nearby fields, cautioning them not to go out of sight of the house.

'There is a pretty, little stream you could follow,' she suggested. 'But look out for Scotsmen or Cromwell's soldiers — they're both as bad as one another. And if you see Charles Stuart, wish him well from me!'

'We wouldn't know him if we saw him!' Dorothy laughed.

'My brother saw him before he had to flee to France when his father was defeated. A very tall lad, he said, with black hair. Rather ugly, he told me, but with a charming way about him.'

Beth had been busy tying her cloak ribbons, but her fingers grew still as she listened to Meg. An idea formed in her mind. She shook her head. It was a foolish thought, she decided, and finished fastening her cloak.

Dorothy chattered about their experiences and Aunt Elizabeth as they wandered along by the stream, and did not notice at first how quiet her companion was. When she did, she thought Beth was probably worrying about her mother, and talked in a kind-hearted attempt to distract her.

They had been walking about an hour and were thinking of returning to the house when they heard the noise of a group of horsemen riding fast along the road. Mindful of Meg's warning, they hid themselves by a hedge which concealed them from the riders. Through the bushes they could see the flash of armour, and as the riders came nearer they saw the buff coats and lobster-pot helmets which identified them as a body of Cromwell's men. They kept still and quiet as the soldiers rode past.

'I wonder where they are making for,' Dorothy said. 'They looked as if they were going to a definite place and not just generally looking for Charles's men. I hope they don't find any! I shall never forget how they were treating those poor prisoners yesterday.'

Beth's mind worked fast. The men

were riding towards Moseley Hall, and riding purposefully, as Dorothy said. She remembered the small group of men they had passed yesterday evening, and Meg's description of a tall, dark man. She looked around wildly. If she ran across the fields, surely she could reach the Hall and give a warning before the soldiers got there!

Making up her mind, she turned to the younger girl.

'Dorothy, go back to Aunt Elizabeth. I've got to go to Moseley Hall. Tell Aunt Elizabeth that I'll explain later when I return!'

Before Dorothy could make any protest, Beth was already running lightly across the meadow, leaving Dorothy to look helplessly after her.

9

Beth sped over the fields, trying to conceal herself from any watchers on the main road by keeping to the far side of the hedges as she made for Moseley Hall as directly as she could. Now she could see the two tall groups of chimneys on its roof, and then the three gables of the Hall came into view.

Beth raced through the gardens at the back of the house. The heavily-studded back door was open, and she looked round wildly as she entered. Noises were coming from a room almost opposite the door.

Beth twisted the handle, thrust it open, and found herself looking at an elderly woman who was busy stirring a saucepan. She jerked upright at Beth's entrance and looked at the girl in amazement.

'Soldiers!' Beth managed to say.

'They're coming here. You must hide the King!'

The tall countrywoman stood stolidly holding the ladle.

'What's that you say?'

Beth could have wept. Every second counted, and this woman's slowness was wasting time!

'A party of Cromwell's men are on their way here to search the house. You must hide the King before they arrive!'

The woman continued to look at her blankly.

'What king? What are you talking about?'

Beth became aware of a dreadful uncertainty. Suddenly she felt weak and doubtful. She had been so sure that the tall, dark man she had seen making for the Hall yesterday must have been the King. But her belief had been based on a glimpse when the light was failing and Meg's casual remarks.

Now she had made a fool of herself, and, what was worse, had revealed her active Royalist sympathies to a household which might betray her to the authorities.

Then her heart leaped as she noticed how the maid had edged closer to the long, wooden table in the centre of the room. She had abandoned the ladle, and her hand was stealing toward the handle of a fearsome kitchen knife which lay there.

The woman was afraid, and not for herself. She could not be afraid of Beth, even if she thought she was mad, for she was tall and strong, and Beth would have been no match for her. So who was she eager to protect?

Beth took a deep breath and stood upright. At her second attempt she managed to speak calmly.

'My name is Beth Henchley, and my father, Richard Henchley, died fighting for the late King Charles at Newby Bridge. Now I want to help his son. I know he is here because I saw him making his way to this house yesterday with three other men.'

The maid and Beth looked at each other steadily for a long moment, and then Beth was pushed aside and she heard the older woman urgently calling up the stairs.

'Master Whitgreave! Soldiers! Soldiers are coming!'

Beth heard an exclamation and rapid movement from somewhere in the house, and then the maid returned to the kitchen and shut the door.

'Here — take this ladle and stir the soup. You're a maid here, and if they ask, you haven't seen any strangers during the last few days. Wait! Put this apron on so you look the part.'

With that she sat down at the table and calmly started to prepare vegetables with the knife which she had been ready to use as a weapon minutes earlier. Beth dutifully began to stir the soup, but started and almost dropped the ladle as she heard the noise of horses at the front of the house. The soldiers had come, but with any luck they would be too late.

Then there was the sound of steady footsteps crossing the hall and the front door was opened. There was a shout of triumph from the horsemen. Beth and the maid abandoned their pretence at housekeeping and stole out into the hall, from where they could peer out to see what was happening. A quietly-dressed gentleman had been seized by two burly troopers who held him tightly by the arms in front of a mounted officer.

'One of Charles Stuart's men!' the officer declared. 'And when did you run from Worcester? When we drove you back to the city by push of pike, or when we stormed the town?'

'You are mistaken,' the gentleman protested, making no attempt to resist the rough handling the troopers were giving him. 'I was not at Worcester.'

It dawned on Beth that she had been mistaken in one thing. The soldiers had come in pursuit of the master of Moseley Hall, not Charles Stuart!

'Master Whitgreave!' There was menace

in the officer's voice. 'We know that you were once a Royalist officer, and fought as a captain at Naseby. Your Catholic sympathies are well known. Are you trying to tell us that you didn't go to help Charles and his Scottish rabble?'

'I can assure you that I have not helped Charles Stuart in his campaign and I was not at the recent battle,' Thomas Whitgreave said calmly. 'I have been ill for some time, and have not left my house. Ask my neighbours.'

By this time passers-by and neighbours had formed a group of onlookers, eager to find out what was happening. Now there was a murmur of agreement, and a man who looked like a prosperous farmer strode forward.

'Thomas Whitgreave is speaking the truth, officer. He has been too weak to leave his bed, and could never have been at Worcester. My wife called to see how he was and brought him some of her lavender oil on that day.'

The officer looked at him angrily but ignored what he said, until other voices were raised to confirm his information.

'He may have deceived you, but he's a Royalist and a traitor, and we're taking him back to Worcester gaol to join his friends!' the officer insisted.

But more and more people assured him that Whitgreave had not left his house for some weeks, giving details of when they had seen him. Whatever they thought of his political and religious sympathies, they were not having a good neighbour unjustly arrested at the whim of the military.

Finally the officer could not ignore their evidence any more, and had to yield to their protests.

'Let him go!' he ordered his troopers reluctantly.

The troopers released their grip on the prisoner, but instead of retreating into the security of his house, Thomas Whitgreave stood in the road rubbing his arms where they had held him. With his open front door behind him, he was a picture of innocence with nothing to hide, and he remained in the road until the soldiers had ungraciously retreated along the road in defeat. He still stood stubbornly outside for some time after that.

'What is he doing?' Beth whispered.

'Making sure they've really gone,' the maid said with a sour laugh.

Finally, Whitgreave, thanking his neighbours for their support, came back into the hall, closing the front door behind him. He stood there for a while, looking pale and drawn.

It was clear that this experience, coming on top of his illness, had taxed his strength almost to breaking-point, but he gave the maid a shaky smile.

'All's well, Jane, for the moment at least.'

Then he turned to Beth.

'I must thank you for the warning you gave. It took courage to act as you did, and I am sure that everyone in this house is equally grateful.'

There was a slight stress on 'everyone'. Then, wearily, he began to climb the stairs to give his news to whoever waited on the upper floors.

'Wasn't he brave!' Beth exclaimed to Jane in the kitchen. 'He just stood there, with those great brutes holding him, as calm as you please!'

Jane looked at her proudly.

'I've known Thomas Whitgreave since he was a small boy. I knew those Roundheads wouldn't get the better of him! And in my opinion it takes more nerve to be brave on your own than in battle when you're charging along with all your friends beside you!'

Then she changed the subject, remembering how Beth's father had died.

'Now tell me more about where you come from and how you knew we needed warning.'

Beth explained her situation hastily, and ended in anxious tones.

'I'd better go. Mistress Everard and Dorothy will be worried about me.'

But Jane was shaking her head.

'You will have to stay here a bit longer,' she said. 'Some of those soldiers may still be lurking about, spying to see if they can accuse us of anything else. The gardener is going to take Mistress Everard some mutton she wanted, so he can take a message to say you are safe and well, but he's too old and feeble to offer you much protection if you went with him. Then, when we are sure all the rascals are safely out of the way, we'll have you escorted safely home.'

She bustled out the back, and returned a few minutes later looking shocked and indignant.

'The miserable, sneaking villains! While we thought all the soldiers were with the master out front, one of them had slipped round to the yard where the blacksmith was busy with the horses and offered him a thousand pounds if he could tell him where the king was! Fortunately the blacksmith knew nothing, for such a great amount of money must be a strong temptation to a poor man.'

The next few hours were a dull

anti-climax for Beth. Jane was friendly enough and fed her well, but in spite of the fact that she now appeared to trust her, she did not let her leave the kitchen, and told her nothing of who might be in the house beside Thomas Whitgreave. For all she knew, Beth thought, Whitgreave might be shielding some obscure friend, and the king might be nowhere near Moseley Hall.

But, as the evening drew in, Master Whitgreave appeared at the kitchen door, looking for Beth.

'I have thanked you already, I know,' he said, 'but I would like to repeat that thanks.'

Beth smiled back shyly and protested that there was no need, but he went on.

'There is another who would like to thank you in person, if you will kindly come with me.'

She followed him into the hall and up to the first floor. There was the sound of voices from behind a shut door, and she looked round.

'It seems safer for us all if you do not

see all our guests and they do not see you,' he said gravely, then he pointed up another flight of stairs.

'I am afraid that our guest can only stretch his legs safely in the attic,' he commented. 'Go through the door at the top. I will wait here.'

Timidly, Beth mounted the stairs and knocked hesitantly on the door.

'Come in!' she heard, and, opening the door, found herself in the presence of her king.

Over the years, Beth had formed a vague, idealised mental picture of the king — a dignified character dressed in velvet and silk, heavily adorned with gold. The reality was a tall, young man with roughly short-cropped dark hair whose face and hands had been stained with walnut juice.

Tom would have disdained the coarse clothes he wore, and it had obviously been difficult to find spare garments to fit him. He was also limping badly — the result of hours of walking in ill-fitting labourer's shoes.

A long nose and wide mouth contributed to a face that could be described as interesting, but could never be called handsome. Then he smiled at her, and her disappointment vanished. Long lashes which a woman might have envied, framed his large, dark eyes and redeemed his other features, and Beth was instantly aware of his great charm.

She sank into a deep curtsey, mentally bewailing the meagre width of her skirts which spoiled its full impressiveness.

'Sire! Your majesty!'

Charles came forward and raised her up by her right hand.

'Madam, any respect is due to you. I understand that you ran considerable risks to warn me that soldiers were on their way. If they had discovered what you had done, you could well be in prison now with so many of my brave followers.'

'It was my duty, whatever the risk. My father died to save the king, and I would have betrayed him if I had not tried to save you.'

'He was a faithful servant of my father's?'

Beth found herself pouring out details of her father's fate, and what had happened since to her mother and herself. His eyes were so warm and sympathetic that she lost all feeling of awe.

'So you can see,' she concluded, 'that I would do anything for you.'

'Anything?' Charles murmured, gently seizing both her hands in his.

'Anything you want of me is yours!' she assured him.

Her mind was full of images of bravery and self-sacrifice. She was deeply shocked, therefore, when instead of thanking her for her devotion to his cause, Charles's arms had gone round her, and he was kissing her in a way that showed no hint of royal dignity.

She struggled to free herself, but Charles was tall and strong. The violent embrace brought back memories of her struggle against the Scottish royalist soldier, and she was filled with revulsion. She could not break his grasp and grew panic-stricken. Then she remembered the limp.

Her respect for royalty and devotion to the House of Stuart forgotten, she ruthlessly stamped hard on his right foot. As he gave a yelp of agony and relaxed his grip, she slapped her king's face as hard as she could.

'Allow me!' a familiar voice said grimly, and she was swept aside. As Charles faced the newcomer in surprise, Tom Everard's fist hit his chin crisply, and Beth saw the king knocked flat on his royal back.

Charles opened his mouth to call for help, and Beth went rigid with fear. What chance would Puritan Tom have against the King's protectors? But Tom stood contemptuously looking down at him.

'Call for help! Why not? Let everyone see what kind of man they are risking their lives for! A king who would try to attack the girl who saved him!'

'You are mistaken, sir. I thought the lady was willing.'

He turned towards her, a reluctant smile on his mobile mouth.

'I confess, when you stamped on my foot and slapped my face, I did begin to wonder if I had made a mistake.'

'I gave you no encouragement!'

'No? 'Anything you want of me is yours,' ' he quoted at her.

'Did you really say that to him?' Tom looked at Beth in amazement.

'I meant anything to help him escape,' she said hotly.

'How was I to know that anyone could be so naïve?' Charles demanded.

'So innocent, you mean.' Tom turned to him challengingly.

The two tall, young men, one fair, one dark, confronted each other. Then Charles smiled. This time it was not the practised smile of a conscious charmer but showed genuine amusement, and some shame.

'You are right, and I must ask

forgiveness of the lady.'

Under Tom's wary gaze, he advanced to Beth and took her reluctant hand. She tried to tug it away but he held it firmly and bent to kiss it.

'Please forgive me,' he said gravely. 'I have grown cynical over the past few years. Too many women have been too willing to accept the advances of a king, even if he is penniless and without a throne.'

Beth blushed scarlet, and mumbled something which he apparently took for an acceptance of his apology, for his attention returned to Tom.

'I am curious to know why you came here. Were you coming to help me, before the lady took precedence?'

'My support is for Parliament,' Tom stated, 'though I may have given your supporters downstairs another impression. But you may rest easy. My first concern is the safety of Mistress Henchley here, and I cannot expose you without revealing what she has done for you.

'Anyway, I have no great wish to see you captured. After Worcester, you are no threat to the peace of England. All I want to do is see Beth safe.'

'Then I can show my gratitude for what Mistress Henchley did for me by seeing my friends let you pass safely.' Charles looked at them with wry amusement. 'I will come downstairs and assure them you may go.'

He started towards the door, and then paused.

'First, may I know your name?'

'Thomas Everard,' Tom returned proudly.

'A name I shall try to remember.'

'Surely you won't hold a grudge against him!' Beth said, shocked. 'He was protecting me!'

She blinked in spite of herself as Charles turned the full force of his charming smile on her.

'By no means. But when I return as king I will need honest men, whatever their beliefs.'

Tom lifted a sceptical eyebrow.

'Do you really think you will ever rule England?'

The smile faded, and Charles looked at him with great seriousness.

'Oh, yes,' he said softly. 'I must believe it. The life of a poor and landless king is very miserable. I must believe that some day I will be welcomed back to England.'

10

Thomas Whitgreave waited at the bottom of the stairs, but he was now accompanied by a well-built man whose hand rested on his sword hilt. Beth remembered the voices she had heard. There were reinforcements available if they were needed to stop Tom.

'The young man insisted you were expecting him, Your Majesty, and seemed to know all about the lady. Is he indeed a friend?'

Thomas Whitgreave's face showed again how much strain the responsibility for the king's safety was putting on him.

But Charles Stuart, descending behind Tom, did not hesitate. His voice was calm and reassuring.

'He was right and there is no need for weapons. Master Everard has come to escort Mistress Henchley safely back to his great-aunt's house. With so many of Cromwell's troops in the area, the lady may need a strong arm to protect her from any — unexpected — threats.'

At the back door, the maid waited with Beth's cloak. She wrapped it round the girl, and then gave her an unexpected kiss on the cheek.

'You're a brave girl as well as a pretty one,' she said. 'Take care!'

As they started to walk along the road, Tom gave a shuddering sigh, and Beth sensed the tension within him relax.

'I was wondering if I would get out of that nest of Royalists alive!' he said with deep feeling.

'Oh, Tom! I was so glad to see you! But why were you here? Has something happened to my mother? How did you know what was happening?'

'Your mother is the same as when you left. When the grooms returned they told my father that he had made a mistake, that south of Worcester was full of fleeing Scots and soldiers hunting for Charles Stuart. He sent me to check what the situation was, and whether it was safe for you both to stay.'

'But what about the king and Moseley Hall?'

'When I reached my aunt's they told me about the message that Master Whitgreave had sent. Not before time, either. Both of them had been frantically worried about you. When I heard everything I wondered whether you were possibly trying to help some Royalist, or even your king.

'When I got to the Hall I bluffed, implying that whatever was happening I knew all about it. I told them that I knew the king was there, so there was no use denying it, and that I had to see him at once.

'It wasn't difficult. After all, there was little danger in letting an unarmed man in. I knew that it would be getting out that would be the trouble.'

'I must thank you . . . '

'No need. Let's get back. It's growing cold.'

They walked on in silence. Beth's feelings were a maelstrom of conflicting emotions. Earlier that day she had experienced fear, then pride and happiness in what she had done. Disillusionment had followed. The king she had dreamed of was a lecherous and unprincipled man, in spite of his charm. Now Tom, who had saved her from shame twice, was as cold to her as to a stranger.

She knew why, of course. He saw her as a foolish girl for whom he had twice risked his life. She was a nuisance, a burden, and obviously all Tom wanted to do was to return home and to Mistress Clarissa Farnwell, probably, the fair and eligible young lady.

A sob escaped her. Tom stopped.

'What now?'

She started to say that nothing was the matter, that she was tired and wanted to get back to her bed as soon as possible, but then bit her lip. Suddenly it seemed to her overwhelmingly important that Tom, who had been her trusted friend for so long, should understand her actions.

He had to realise that she was not just a stupid blunderer. So she stood in the moonlight, her old cloak clasped round her against the chill, autumn dews, and faced him.

'Tom, I'm sorry beyond words for the trouble I have caused you, and I am more grateful than I can say for the way you rescued me. But I believe in the monarchy. My father died for it, and although I'm only a girl, and we are supposed to leave all such matters to men, I had to help Charles Stuart. Otherwise, my beliefs, my father's sacrifice, would have meant nothing. I would have betrayed my faith, my dream.'

Tom's face was still and unreadable as he looked down at her.

'I understand your ideals, I admire your courage.' Here a note of exasperation entered his voice. 'But do you have to practically offer yourself to a libertine who took his first mistress when he was fourteen and has already fathered at least one child?'

Beth was temporarily distracted from political ideals by this information.

'Fourteen! And he has a child?' she exclaimed in disbelief.

For a moment the old Tom appeared as he said with a mixture of horror and amusement, 'I shouldn't have said that to a young maid! Don't repeat it to Dorothy, or my father will flay me!'

Then he shrugged his shoulders.

'His first woman was a Lady Wyndham, if you must know. Apparently she was once one of his nurses! And he has a son, James, whom he adores, by Lucy Walters. That is your king! Beth, how are we getting distracted by scandal-mongering?'

She considered what he had said, frowning a little.

'He may not be faultless, but he is still the king, God's anointed.'

'Your anointed king seemed to be suffering considerably at your hands, and feet, when I arrived. You scarcely needed rescuing, Mistress Henchley!'

It was too dark to see her blush, but she drew herself up with what dignity she could muster.

'As he said, I appeared to have misled him.'

Then her dignity collapsed, and she stood forlornly, tears in her eyes.

'Oh, Tom! What can I do now? Even if my mother recovers, she and I are paupers. The king's cause is lost and he is not worth fighting for anyway. I have nothing left to believe in or hope for. What can I do?'

He stretched out a finger and gently wiped the tears from her cheek.

'It seems to me there is only one thing you can do,' he said carefully. 'You must marry me.'

She blinked incredulously.

'What?' she enquired baldly.

He sighed.

'I am not prepared to keep wandering the country at night, rescuing you from all types of situations. If you marry me I can look after you and protect you from your wild ideas. And

181

Hatchford Manor will be a comfortable home for you and your mother.'

Beth looked at him silently, at his tall figure. The moonlight shone on the planes of his face, emphasised their dignity and resolution. She realised that maturity was transforming him into a handsome man as well as a good man.

Her beloved Tom! She loved him not only as a friend, she suddenly realised, but as a man. That was why she had detested Clarissa Farnwell so much. It had been the jealousy of a woman who sees a favoured rival. And now he was offering her marriage.

She thought rapidly. If she accepted him, her troubles would be over.

'No!'

'What?'

There was desperation as well as disbelief in Tom's exclamation.

'At least pretend to think about it!'

'No!' she said firmly.

'Don't be silly! It will solve all your problems!'

'No!' she repeated yet again, and

then suddenly flared into fury at him, her fists tightly clenched in anger.

'How dare you insult me!'

'Insult you?' he cried indignantly, as bewildered as she was furious. 'I've asked you to marry me!'

'Out of pity! So you can stop me getting into trouble, like a tutor looking after a naughty child! Isn't that an insult?'

Tom had succeeded in grasping her wrists tightly, and now held her at arm's length.

'Calm down, Beth. I think we'd better talk!'

'I've no wish to talk to you any more,' she raged. He held her at a safe distance as she kicked vainly at him as hard as she could. 'Take me back to your aunt's house immediately, and then you can go and offer marriage to Clarissa Farnwell. Perhaps she'll have you!'

'Clarissa Farnwell? What has she got to do with me?' He stood for some seconds, still holding Beth's wrists.

Then he seemed to come to a decision.

'Very well, let's have the truth. I'm not offering to marry you out of pity. I love you. I am tired of playing protector and rescuing you from other men's kisses, because the truth is — I want to kiss you myself. I know you regard me as a brother, but it's some time since I've thought of you as a sister!'

He had released her wrists as he spoke, and she stood rubbing them, her mouth trembling.

'Why didn't you tell me?'

'Because I knew you didn't think of me as I thought of you. I love you so much, Beth. I want to kiss you and hold you, but also I want you as my wife, to share my whole life.'

It took her two short steps to cover the space between them. Her cloak slid back as she raised her arms and clasped him round the neck.

'Show me,' she said softly, and his arms went round her as he bent his head to hers.

She felt the tender firmness of his

184

lips. His long fingers pressed against her back, bringing her against his warm body. It was Tom who broke the embrace, lifting his lips from hers and holding her away from him. Beth smiled at him, her happiness clear in the light of the moon.

'I've reconsidered,' she said. 'I will marry you.'

'So I should hope,' he returned a little huskily. 'Out alone with a young man at past midnight! Only marriage can save your reputation now, my girl.'

She rested her head on his chest, feeling utterly safe, cherished and protected by the friend who had suddenly become her love. For a few moments he murmured endearments into her soft hair before resolutely taking her hand and setting off at a fast pace.

'I think it best we get home now,' he said in reply to her protests. 'I'm not sure my Puritan upbringing can withstand the combination of you and the moonlight!'

A small side door had been left unfastened for them at Millfeld House, and they slipped in as silently as possible. At the foot of the stairs they stopped, and stood locked in each other's arms in a final kiss.

'Good-night, my love,' Tom whispered. 'I must make the door secure.'

As she crept up the stairs in stockinged feet, Beth did not see a small figure gently close one of the bedroom doors. Mistress Elizabeth Everard went back to her bed with a happy heart.

Beth stripped her clothes off quickly and slid in beside Dorothy. The younger girl half-woke and mumbled an enquiry.

'It's all right. Tom and I are both safe. I'll tell you all about it in the morning,' Beth whispered, and Dorothy sank back to sleep.

Beth herself felt that she would never sleep again. The day's events and the future were too exciting. But she had not realised how exhausted she was, and soon she was fast asleep.

Beth woke in the morning to find the sun high in the sky and Dorothy's side of the bed empty. She made a hasty toilet and hurried down the broad stairs and when she looked into the morning parlour she saw Tom standing by the window.

At the sight of his tall figure she halted abruptly, suddenly overcome by shyness. In the cold light of day it was difficult to believe in the fairy-tale of the previous night. He looked at her solemnly at first, as if her friend of so many years was unsure how to greet her. Then he smiled and held out his hands, and their kiss reassured her that the passion of the previous night had not faded.

'Mistress Everard thought it best to let you sleep on,' he explained. 'I waited to see you before I left.'

'You're going back so soon?' she said in dismay. 'But I want to be with you! Can I come, too?'

'I hate to leave you,' he said tenderly, 'but I promised to let my parents know how things are here as quickly as possible. And now I shall have extra news to tell them.'

Beth looked down, a tiny frown forming.

'Will your parents be very upset when they learn that their only son wants to marry a penniless girl?'

She looked up indignantly as he laughed.

'When I said my father sent me here, perhaps it would have been truer to say that I insisted on coming. And from something he has said, I don't believe my parents will be altogether surprised at the news, and they certainly won't be distressed. Beth, my darling idiot, they've regarded you almost as their daughter ever since you came to Hatchford. Now I'm making you truly their daughter, and they'll be delighted.'

'Are you sure that's true?' She looked at him wistfully.

He kissed her by way of reply, and so Mistress Everard and Dorothy found them as they came in from the garden.

Beth and Dorothy stayed at Millfeld House for three weeks, partly to please Aunt Elizabeth and partly to let the countryside settle down after Worcester. Tom came to escort the the girls home, bringing with him letters from Sir Thomas Everard and his wife that convinced Beth at last that they would welcome her as Tom's wife.

The return journey was uneventful. Cromwell's soldiers had captured most of the Royalist fugitives from Worcester, though there was still no news of what had happened to Charles Stuart.

When the little party arrived at Hatchford Manor, both Sir Thomas and Lady Everard were waiting at the open door, and came forward to greet the three young people. Tom's mother greeted her with a kiss and a warm hug. Sir Thomas did the same, then smiled happily down at her.

A little while later, Beth went up to see her mother. Mary sat by the bed, sewing, and her face lit up at the sight of Beth. Mistress Henchley seemed to have aged but there was sanity in her look. When Beth, sitting by the bed and holding her mother's hand, started to tell her about Tom and herself, she was apprehensive about her mother's reaction. But her mother nodded and said that she had already learned the news from Lady Everard.

'It is a good match for you, Beth. You have my blessing. Lying here, I have come to realise how ungrateful I have been to the Everards. All these years I have ignored what they were doing for us. Of course, I regret that they have different loyalties, but Sir Thomas was your father's friend.'

Beth kissed her mother with tears in her eyes, immeasurably relieved by the fact that she had accepted the engagement, and not forced Beth to choose between her mother and Tom.

★   ★   ★

Tom and Beth were married at Hatchford Church two months later by

the gentle old vicar whom Sir Thomas
had chosen to fill the place of the dead
Werham. Beth's mother attended the
service, though she never fully recovered in mind or body from the blow to
her head. Mary nursed her devotedly,
and she was cherished and protected by
all the Everards.

A year later, she was well enough to
hold Beth's firstborn son in her arms,
and her thin face glowed with pride
when she learned that he was to be
named Richard after his maternal
grandfather.

The following morning, Mary found
her cold in her bed. She had died
peacefully in her sleep, and clasped in
her hand was the locket with the dark
curl of her husband's hair which Sir
Thomas Everard had brought back
from Newby Bridge.

Charles Stuart had to wait some time
for his dream to be fulfilled, but in
1660 England sent for her king at last.
Until then, he had been in exile in
France. Although he was unreliable in

so many matters, he showed his gratitude to those who helped him escape after Worcester, and Thomas Whitgreave received an annuity.

Beth saw him once more when he visited the Worcester area. She sat with the rest of the prosperous Everard family at a window looking down at the scene as the mayor welcomed the king to the town where he had once been a royal fugitive. Again she saw his tall figure, this time finely-dressed and moving with lazy grace.

His gaze passed over her, without recognising the elegant matron in tawny satin with gold ribbons as the young girl who had once raced to save his life. Moseley Hall seemed part of another world. She smiled with deep contentment at her fair-haired husband, and saw in his eyes the love that had never faltered. That, she thought, had been the true dream.